SOPHIE WASHINGTON
CLASS RETREAT

D0168889

BY

TONYA DUNCAN ELLIS

Other Books by
Tonya Duncan Ellis

Sophie Washington: Queen of the Bee

Sophie Washington: The Snitch

Sophie Washington:
Things You Didn't Know About Sophie

Sophie Washington: The Gamer

Sophie Washington: Hurricane

Sophie Washington: Mission: Costa Rica

Sophie Washington: Secret Santa

Sophie Washington: Code One

Sophie Washington: Mismatch

Sophie Washington: My BFF

Contents

CHAPTER ONE

Big Foot

A twig snaps, and the dark shadow rises. I run like a rabbit through leafy trees. My hair is drenched; I can smell the sweat in my armpits. Down, down, down the trail I race for dear life. As the footsteps get closer, I turn. A tall, hairy man grabs my arm, and I scream.

Heart racing, I jerk up and pull my comforter to my chest. I see my goldfish bowl on my dresser and breathe a sigh of relief. It's the third night in a row I've had nightmares about Big Foot. I hope they stop soon because this is getting old.

The dreams started after I watched a show called *Finding Big Foot* with my parents and little brother, Cole. I want to forget about the hairy ape man, also known as Sasquatch. But Cole's been talking about it every chance he gets. This morning, unfortunately, is no different.

"What do you call a Sasquatch who loves working with clay?" Cole reads a joke from his library book. "A hairy potter!"

"What do you get when Bigfoot walks in your garden? "Squash!"

"It's too early for this!" I put my hands over my ears. I should have packed my ear plugs in my bag with my swimsuit.

My father laughs as he pulls into our school entrance. With the orange and pinkish colors of the sun coming up from behind the clouds, the two-story, gray building stands out like a piece in a pop-up book. About twenty or thirty other cars are sliding into parking spaces, and I strain my eyes to find my friends.

"Did you know that Big Foot's feet are 24 inches long?" Cole asks. "I wonder what size shoes he wears?"

"Pretty big ones, since I'm a size 12 and my feet are 11 inches," says Dad.

"Big Foot lives in the woods and is nocturnal. That means he comes out at night." Cole continues. "You'd better be careful on your trip, Sophie."

"I'm sure the chaperones will keep your sister safe." Mom glances through the rearview mirror, crinkles of laughter around her eyes.

My sixth-grade class is going on a retreat, a once-a-year tradition at Xavier Academy. Two whole days of eating s'mores, swimming, and hanging with my friends, without my eight-year-old brother and his Big Foot talk.

The retreat is at Camp Glowing Spring, which has a lake, pool, cabins, and a hiking trail. I'll get to stay up late, eat burgers and pizza, and spend hours with my besties. I can't wait!

"If you see a tall, hairy man moving through the trees, run!" warns Cole. "Big Foot isn't known to attack humans, but you can't be too careful."

"I'd never be in the woods by myself." I shift my body under my seatbelt so I can face Cole directly. "And since there is no such thing as Big Foot, I don't have to worry about seeing it."

"I wish you could bring your cell phone so you could take a picture if Big Foot comes out." Cole ignores my argument. "Then we could prove all the naysayers wrong."

"I'm one of them, silly. I don't believe in ghosts or Big Foot!"

"It's all in fun, Sophie." Mom reaches over the seat for my hand, and I look out the window, pretending I don't see her.

We all know good and well that Big Foot doesn't exist. I'm not acting like it does to make Cole happy. Mom and Dad take his side on *everything*. He's always spoiling my fun. Last weekend, I missed a sleepover with my friends because they had to work and wanted me to play with him. Cole's always tagging along when I go somewhere.

He's just trying to scare me with all this Big Foot nonsense, and I'm not having it.

Thankfully, Cole gets quiet as he runs his fingers across the page to read about more monsters.

The biscuit I ate this morning feels like lead in my stomach as we circle around the lot one last time. Other people get out and stand by their cars, and I wring my hands. I wish Dad would find a parking spot already.

When a gray car pulls in, I pop up like a piece of toast.

"There's Chloe!" I tap my fingernail on the glass.

My BFF slides out of her parents' car, lugging a large, brightly-colored duffle bag, pillow, and blanket. Spotting our other friend Valentina, she shrieks, and they skip to each other and hug.

"Calm down, Sophie," says my father, as I bounce in my seat. "You'll be on your way soon enough."

"I wish you were this excited to go to school every day," Mom says with a laugh.

I wish the *entire* family hadn't come to drop me off. My parents treat me like such a baby sometimes.

"Hey, Sophie, is that what you're riding in?" Cole tugs on my tee shirt sleeve and points out a muddy school bus pulling in. "It doesn't look so good."

The paint is faded and peeling in some areas, and the windshield is so dusty it's a wonder the driver can see out of it.

"Where on earth did the school get that thing from?" asks Mom, as the bus screeches to a stop.

"I don't know." Dad stops in front of an empty parking space, and then turns back to me. "But if this is your transportation, you might be staying home."

Stay home and miss class retreat?! That would be scarier than seeing Sasquatch! Pa-lease let the bus work okay.

CHAPTER TWO

Tag-A-Long

The next couple of minutes seem like an hour as Dad backs into a space on the second row and turns off the engine. We get out of the car, and he helps me with my bag.

"Is Sophie still going, Daddy?" I glare at my little brother and make a zip your lip gesture near my mouth. He's always messing things up.

Near the loading dock, Mr. Quackenbush, my tennis coach, walks up to the dirty bus and speaks to the driver. The driver pulls out a piece of paper and shows it to the coach. After glancing at the sheet, Coach Quackenbush gestures to the back of the school with his clipboard.

"That other bus is driving away, Dad!" I yell when the mud-caked vehicle leaves the parking lot. Two shiny, newer buses ease in its place, and a weight leaves my chest.

"Parents, say your goodbyes at your cars please!" Coach Quackenbush's nasal voice rumbles through a megaphone. "We'd like all students to gather to the right with their class groups. We will be loading up to leave in approximately twenty minutes."

"Give me my hug now, young lady." Mom pulls me so close I can barely breathe. "We're going to miss you, sweetie!"

Though it's only 6:30 in the morning the air already feels sticky. It will probably be another hot Texas day.

"Be careful, follow the teacher and chaperones' instructions, and stay with the group at all times." Dad says before kissing my cheek. "We love you!"

"Love you, too, Mom and Dad! See you on Friday!"

"Can I stay with Sophie while you sign her in?" asks Cole. I give him the side eye.

"That's a great idea!" Mom glances over at the long line of parents by the bus. "Stay with your sister a minute, and we'll come get you before we leave."

I want to complain, but I bite my bottom lip and don't say anything. I've been excited about this trip for weeks, and nothing is going to bring me down.

"You're walking too fast, Sophie!" Cole hop skips to keep up as I push through the crowd toward my friends. I ignore him.

We wind through the maze of kids, and I nod at some of them. Since I started at Xavier in kindergarten and am in a lot of activities, I know most of the sixth graders. My parents say I worry too much about what everybody thinks about me, but they just don't understand. I like being in the popular crowd. School is much more fun when you have friends.

"Ouch! A bug bit me!" Cole hops up and down like he's got ants in his pants, and Carlos and Brandon from 6B point and laugh. How embarrassing!

"Will you shush!" I fuss. "You're always acting silly!"

"I didn't do anything." Cole stares at the concrete with his lip poked out.

"Don't be mad, Cole. I'm sorry."

I pat his back and glance over to where my parents are standing. If they notice he's upset, I'll be in big trouble. Whenever we have a disagreement they swoop in to save Cole like Wonder Woman and Superman.

"Sophie!"

I let out a breath as my BFF, Chloe, sees us and runs over with a hug.

"Hey, Cole, what's up?"

He gives a small smile and returns her fist bump. Like all the other boys, my little brother has a serious crush on Chloe. It's not hard to understand why.

She's never-need-a-filter pretty with smooth skin and every hair in place. Chloe's super sweet most of the time too, unless you tease her about being dyslexic, so I guess she's what my Dad would call the "perfect catch."

"Riding on the bus is going to be so fun!" Chloe waves her hands in front of her face like a music conductor. "I downloaded some new songs to listen to on my cell phone."

"Si, amigas! I cannot wait!"

Valentina bounces up to us, her long, straight black hair streaming behind. The captain of the cheerleading squad my friends and I are all members of, she's usually full of energy.

"Anybody want a churro?" She holds out a brown paper bag filled with sugary, cinnamon treats.

"Thanks! Your grandma's churros are the best!" I reach in the bag and grab one. "Yummy! These are still warm."

"Can I have a one too?" begs Cole.

"Oh, course, amigo. Your little brother is sooo cute, Sophie." Valentina pats his tight curls the same way I pet my dog Bertram.

Cole glows in the spotlight. I cross my arms. I wish my little brother would get a life. These are *my* friends, and he's always barging in.

"Did you bring the shaving cream, Chloe?" Valentina gives a sneaky grin.

"What's that for?" I ask.

"Pranks," says Chloe. "We're going to play tricks on the boys at retreat."

"Do you think that's a good idea?" I frown.

"Oh course! It'll be fabuloso!" says Valentina.

I hope we don't get in trouble. Lately, my friends have been wanting to hang around the boys in our class more. I'm not sure if I like it.

"Looks like they are loading up, guys!" Chloe nods toward the buses. "Come on! Hey, Mariama, over here!" She gestures to our other close friend, who just walked up.

I admire the wooden beaded necklace she's wearing. Mariama's hair is styled in cute, thin braids close to her scalp, with loose afro puffs at the ends. She joined our school last year, after her family moved to Houston from Nigeria. Though I haven't known her as long as I've known Chloe, we're still really close.

"You'd better get with Mom and Dad, Cole." I point over to where they are standing with the other parents.

"But I want to stay with you until you leave, Sophie," he whines.

"Your little brother loves to spend time with you," says Chloe. "That's so sweet."

Sweet enough to give me a stomachache. I smile with all my teeth. I'll be glad when the bus starts rolling! Two whole days without my brother sticking to me like a Band-Aid. I can't wait!

CHAPTER THREE

I Spy

Coach Quackenbush calls out bus assignments from his megaphone. I'm happy my friends and I are grouped together. My mom drives me to school every day, since private schools like Xavier don't have their own buses. It'll be cool to spend extra time with my besties. The kids from 6B and their chaperones are in the second bus.

"See you in a few days!" I wave out the window to my family once I take my seat.

Mom blows one last kiss, and Cole, who Dad came and got while we were in line, jumps up and down.

"Bye, Sophie!"

We're almost on our way!

The sun is fully up, and it's at least 85 degrees outside. It seems even hotter inside the bus. A few of the windows are lowered to let in a breeze. After taking roll from the list on his clipboard the coach sits down in front near the other chaperones. Our seats are in the back.

Only thirty-five people are on the bus, so a few kids and teachers have seats to themselves. We have plenty of extra space for our bags too. As we drive out of the parking lot, I feel like I've been let out of math class for recess. This is going to be a great escape!

"Let's get this party started!" Toby, the cutest boy in our grade, pulls out a pair of sunglasses and slips them on. He and our other classmate, Nathan, are in the seat in front of me and Chloe, and Valentina and Mariama are across the aisle.

Toby pushes in his ear buds and rocks his body from side to side to the beat of the music he's listening to.

"Do you mind? I'm trying to finish this chapter." Nathan frowns, flipping through a big textbook on his lap.

"It's class retreat...why are you studying?" Toby looks over his shades at the book and frowns.

"There's over two hours until we get to the campground." Nathan glares at him through his dark rimmed glasses. "We have a math test on Tuesday after we get back, so I figure I'll get a head start. We're learning about distance, rate, and time. It's actually pretty interesting."

"Sorry, dude. I was just trying to relax." Toby turns the volume down on his phone, looks back at me and Chloe and wags his eyebrows.

"What a nerd." Chloe giggles behind her hand.

I agree that Nathan can go a bit overboard with the studying sometimes. He's super competitive. Last year, he tried to beat me in the school spelling bee, but I won first place there and at regionals.

"You know, you could move closer to the teachers." Toby taps Nathan's shoulder and nods toward the front of the bus. "There're empty seats up there. Who knows, they might give you some extra credit work to do."

"I'm not moving anywhere." Nathan shakes his head. "I have a right to be in this seat as much as you do. You need to stay out of my space."

Nathan slides toward the middle of the seat, and Toby shoves him back.

"Will you two quit fighting?" I sigh. I must admit, I'm impressed at Nathan for standing up to Toby like this. He's the shortest boy in our class, and Toby is a strong basketball star.

The two boys have an on-again, off-again friendship. Sometimes they like each other, sometimes they argue like cats and dogs. One-on-one, I like talking to Nathan, but for some reason he acts weird when we're all together in a group. Chloe says he's jealous that I used to have a crush on Toby, but I'm not into all that boy crazy stuff like she and Valentina are, so I'm not sure.

"Ewww! Nasty!" The boys stop fussing when Mariama holds up a bag with what looks like a month-old sandwich, that had been wedged near the wall.

"This bus is muy gross." Valentina wrinkles her nose.

The bus is bright and shiny on the outside, but inside, it's a mess. Stuffing spills from the side of a few of the cracked leather seats, and there are old candy wrappers and chips bags near the wall on the floor. It has a sweaty, musty odor, like Cole's socks after he plays basketball.

"I might need a book of my own to study, so I won't see all this junk." Mariama throws the trash in the empty area behind their seat.

"You're right, Mariama." Chloe sits up straighter as if that will protect her from germs.

"Chill out," says Toby. "It's not that bad. You guys are too picky."

Giving up on studying, Nathan sets his book in his backpack on the floor. "This bus *does* seem old. My dad told me a company that was closing donated it to the school last year. I hope they've checked to make sure it runs well."

"What do you mean?" I ask. "Our teachers wouldn't have us in a bus that has something wrong with it, would they?"

"You never know," says Nathan. "Since Xavier is small, they don't always have money to pay for things like public schools do."

"Settle down back there!" Coach Quackenbush screams as a paper airplane zooms toward us from the front of the bus.

"Yeah, you're disturbing his shows," says Chloe with a laugh. With their heads lowered, scrolling through their electronic tablets, it seems like the chaperones want downtime as much as we do.

We've driven out of the Houston city limits and are now in the countryside. Fields of cut, green grass stretch out for miles on each side of the bus. A giant oil pump that looks like a hammer attached to a spring moves up and down. I wonder how many gallons of oil it drills per day.

"Let's play a game," Valentina suggests. "How about *I Spy*?"

"That's so lame!" Toby grumbles. "We played that on road trips when I was two."

"Come on, Toby! Don't be a spoilsport." Chloe punches his arm over the seat. "It's fun." She turns her head and squints out the open window.

"I spy with my little eye, something red!"

"A stop sign!" yells Valentina.

"No, it's that pickup truck!" I point out the window.

"A convertible!" says Mariama.

"You got it right!" Chloe punches her fist in the air.

"Okay, you pick something, Mariama."

"I spy with my little eye...something green."

"Now, that's too easy!" grumbles Toby. "Look at all that grass out there!"

A pair of steer with wide, handle-bar-like horns on their heads stand behind a barbed wire fence in the bright field. Bushy trees block the scenery behind them.

"You're wrong, Toby! I'm not looking at grass." Mariama shakes her head.

"I know! It's the green roof on that barn over there!" Nathan calls out.

She gives him the thumbs up to signal he's right, and he takes the lead.

"I spy with my little eye, something yellow!"

I squint. What could be yellow out here in the middle of nowhere? There are a few straggly wildflowers around that might have been gold colored last month but are now brown. I glance behind us and do a double take at a yellow, rectangular shape.

"Wait a minute! Look at that!" I shout, and everyone shifts their eyes toward the windows. The bus that the kids in 6B are on is on the side of the road!

CHAPTER FOUR

Old Town Road

"Turn around!" Coach Quackenbush hears the commotion and also notices the stalled bus.

The driver swerves over to the shoulder of the road and then loops back. Chloe almost drops the bottle of orange juice she's pulled from her bag at the jerky movement.

"Geez! This is crazy!" Toby lifts his sunglasses to get a clearer view.

"If that bus doesn't get fixed soon, it might topple over," says Nathan.

The other bus reminds me of the Leaning Tower of Pisa we learned about in history class. One of the back tires sags like a deflated bounce house. The kids from 6B rush out as if it's a burning building. Once outside, they take pictures in front of the bus, while the teachers huddle up near the edge of the road.

Since we're in the middle of nowhere the roads are empty. I wonder if there are any mechanic shops around.

"Get back!" A chaperone yells when Jacob and Carlos try to get a closer look at the collapsed tire. They shuffle toward the rest of the group.

"Whoa!" rumbles the crowd when the bus leans further.

"What are they going to do?" asks Chloe. "Is the other class coming on retreat with us?"

"You know how Xavier always talks about team-work and sticking together." Mariama plays with her necklace. "We'll be lucky if any of us get to go."

What if Mariama is right? My stomach feels like it's being tied in knots. I don't want our trip to be canceled.

"Take your seats, children!" Mr. Bartee, our English teacher, stands up. "We need to assess the situation."

He and Coach Quackenbush climb out and rush over to the other group.

The bus buzzes like bees in a hive as 6A reacts to the breakdown.

"I wonder if that bus has a spare tire," says Nathan.

"It'd be cool if they let us help them change it!" Toby exclaims.

"I'm going to text my mom!" Chloe reaches down for her cell phone. "Oops!"

She knocks over her juice bottle, which she'd set down between us earlier, and it soaks my side of the seat.

"Uggg!" I stand to avoid the cold, wet, stickiness.

"Sorry, Sophie! Let me help!" After picking up the empty bottle from the floor, Chloe tries to wipe up the mess with an extra jacket.

"Oh, no!"

The back of my pants is soaked. I twist around and try to see my bottom. It probably looks like I wet my pants! Luckily, the kids near us are too busy watching what's happening outside the bus to notice. If anybody sees this wet spot on the back of my jeans, I'll never hear the end of it!

"There's Rani! And Mackenzie!" Mariama points out two of our other friends standing together on the grass. Mackenzie shades her eyes from the sun with her hand, and Rani fans herself with a folder.

"Man, I'm glad we aren't in their shoes," says Toby. "It's hot enough on this bus."

"Tell me about it." I pull at my damp tee shirt. It'll be as wet as my jeans if we don't start moving and get a breeze in here soon.

"I'll text Rani to see what the teachers are saying." Chloe taps her phone.

Before she can press send, 6B lines up. Coach Quackenbush boards the bus and pulls out his bullhorn. His sweaty bald head shines like a golden egg.

"The other group is joining us," he booms. "so you need to be two to a seat. A repair crew won't be able to get to the other bus for another hour, and we want to make it to the campgrounds this morning, so we'll still have time for activities."

"That's terrible!" Chloe groans. "Now it'll be even hotter in here."

"And even more crowded," agrees Mariama.

"We need to move, Chloe!" I grip my duffle bag, so we can swap seats. But I'm too late. It's like musical chairs as kids in the front of the bus scramble to sit with their friends, and 6B kids clamor up the steps.

We're stuck in a sopping seat for the next hour and a half.

"Put this under you." She hands me her extra jacket to sit on. "I'll switch sides since it's dryer over here."

Changing places helps, but I still feel uncomfortable. It's going to be a long ride to Camp Glowing Spring.

Once everyone is inside, the door squeaks shut. Coach Quackenbush and Mrs. Waggoner, the lead teacher for the 6B group, take roll again.

"Alright folks! Let's get moving." Coach gets another chance to use his megaphone. "It's a bit tight, but we still have plenty of room. We expect you on your best behavior."

He sits down, and the driver puts the bus in gear. It's like someone turned up a volume dial, as double the number of kids talk to their friends. Christy Chen, a girl who's a star in our school choir, starts singing show tunes, and I wish, again, that I'd packed my ear plugs.

I am not throwing away my shot
I am not throwing away my shot
Hey yo, I'm just like my country
I'm young, scrappy and hungry
And I'm not throwing away my shot

Valentina and Mariama join in the rap song from *Hamilton*, a Broadway movie they saw on television.

This is worse than Cole's corny jokes. I look over the seat to see what the teachers are doing.

Ignoring the noise, they're back to watching movies on their electronic tablets. Nathan picks up his book again, and Toby stares out the window. Chloe scrolls through pictures of her favorite boy band on her phone.

It seems like the *I Spy* game is over, so I close my eyes to take a nap.

CHAPTER FIVE

Camp Glowing Spring

"Wake up, Sophie!" Chloe rubs my shoulder. "We're here."

I twist my stiff neck until it cracks and rub the sleepy stuff from around my eyes. I must've napped for over an hour. My jeans feel drier, thank goodness. I won't have to change my clothes.

The bus tires crunch over gravel as we drive past a white and green billboard that reads "Camp Glowing Spring: Established 1965." The only drawing on the big sign, besides the green letters, is a pine tree with a swirly line around it, which seems like the perfect symbol for this place.

It reminds me of a *Grimm's Fairy Tale* forest, beautiful, but spooky. Giant evergreens surround a long, one-story building, with a lake behind it. The bright sky stretches overhead like a canopy bed. Spanish moss drips from some tree branches like frizzy, gray hair. As we pass a foot trail that winds into the greenery, I shiver, remembering Cole's warnings about Big Foot.

Camp Glowing Spring looks exactly like the woods from my nightmare. What if Big Foot comes to our cabin to get us at night? I blink and shake my head to snap back into reality. *Big Foot is a hoax.* I need to enjoy being away from my little brother's tall tales for the next two days.

As the bus drives deeper into the campground, the hum of excited kids gets louder.

"Check that out!" Toby bounces on his seat and stares at a water park on the lake. There's a wooden pier in the center and an inflatable blue and yellow water slide. A giant-sized, red, yellow, and blue plastic pillow floats beside it.

"That lake is probably 100 feet deep!" Nathan leans over Toby's shoulder.

I wonder what lurks underneath the greenish blue waters. Does Big Foot swim?

"That's the Blob!" Chloe points at the huge, plastic pillow. "Some eighth graders told me how much fun it is. I can't wait to jump out there. If a bigger person flops on after you, your body flies high in the air before you hit the water."

"Cool!" Nathan's eyeballs widen behind his glasses.

I bite my thumbnail.

I'm scared of heights, and the idea of bouncing over a huge lake doesn't exactly float my boat. I better make sure that I'm the last one on the Blob if I do try it.

"That building to the right is the dining hall, where you'll have all your meals." Coach Quackenbush screams through his megaphone. "You'll bus your own tables after breakfast, lunch, and dinner."

"What does bus tables mean?" I glance across the aisle at Mariama.

"We'll be clearing off our own dishes."

At least we won't have to wash them like I do at home.

"We expect you all to be on your best behavior and to follow the rules the camp counselors set." The coach holds up his hand for us to be quiet. "Any funny business and you may have to sit out of activities."

Valentina looks over at Chloe and raises her eyebrow. I hope that means they are giving up on the prank idea. I'll be really mad if we get in trouble joking around with some dumb boys.

"Now that we have all the housekeeping out of the way, let's talk about the fun stuff," the coach continues. "The intent of this retreat is for you to get to know each other better and to bond as a class. As middle school students you are going through many changes with your bodies, friendships, and your schoolwork. Retreat is a time for you to let your hair down and also to gain some independence. Over the next couple of days, we're going to do lots of fun activities like enjoy water sports, archery, campfires, and an optional mud fight. I've been chaperoning these retreats for the past five years and have seen many students grow from the experience."

"Mud fight? What's that all about?" asks Chloe.

"I haven't heard any of the older kids mention it," I say. "It must be something new."

"I'm not going to get in the mud if it's not a requirement." She shakes out her curls.

"Me either." My stomach tightens as we park beside some cabins.

Bouncing in the air, swimming in a lake, mud fights? We're going to be doing lots of dangerous activities the next couple of days. I've been zip lining in Costa Rica on a trip with my family, so I'm not a total Fraidy Cat. But I do get nervous about trying new things sometimes. That lake looked scary. I've never swum in anything except a pool without my folks around.

The bus stops near the dining hall, and we pile out with our bags. It feels great to stretch my legs.

Trees must be like natural air conditioners because the air is cooler out here than it was in Houston. The view looks like a picture post card. Bird song fills the air. Hills and tall, leafy trees stretch on for forever.

"Over here, Sophie! Come on." Chloe waves me over to the rest of the kids.

Nathan and Toby join us and are laughing, so they must have made up on the bus while I was asleep.

"Let's gather for a group photo everybody!" calls Mr. Bartee. "Here, in the clearing-under the trees!"

The trees beside us frame our class as a man with a camp logo tee shirt on snaps a shot with his camera.

"Welcome to Camp Glowing Spring!" calls Coach Quackenbush. "Let the adventure begin!"

CHAPTER SIX

The Counselors

"Take a bathroom break, and then we'll introduce you to your counselors, who will lead you to your cabins." The coach points us toward a restroom area. "Everybody gather back here in ten minutes."

We set our bags by the chaperones and walk into a country-looking log cabin. The boys turn left, and Chloe and I and the other girls go right.

"Why is the girls' bathroom line always longer than the boys'?" she complains as we line up outside the door to wait our turn. "They should give girls more stalls since it takes us more time in there."

"I know, right? It's such a pain."

"There's room for one more." A red-haired girl from 6B slips out seconds later, and Chloe goes in to take her place. For a few minutes, I'm in the hallway by myself.

This cabin reminds me of cowboy shows my grand-dad used to watch. Wooden planks make up the walls and floors, and there are actual logs on the ceiling. There were wood rocking chairs on the front porch entrance that I'd like to try out later if we have time. Are our cabins near here? I glance out a large window at the end of the dark hallway to see if I can get a better view.

Suddenly, the shadow of a tall man, with long scraggly hair and dark, baggy clothes, fills up the floor length pane. I suck in my breath and blink, and he's gone.

That looked like Big Foot! But it couldn't be. I shake my head and press my hands on my cheeks.

"Your turn, Sophie." Chloe and Valentina come out of the restroom a minute later.

I push in the doorway and decide to forget what I just saw. There's no way that was Sasquatch. I'm getting as crazy as Cole.

After everybody finishes, Mr. Bartee comes around with wicker baskets to collect our cell phones and electronics. Most of the kids complain, but I don't mind turning mine in. I'm just happy to be here with my friends.

While Mr. Bartee writes down the phones he's collected in his log book, a youngish man and a short, blond-haired girl walk up to the coach. Valentina blushes, and Chloe tilts her head to the side. Tall, with heavy lashed, gray eyes, the boy reminds me of the lead singer in my best friend's favorite singing group. The tiny girl beside him looks like Tinkerbell.

"He's ca-ute!" Chloe whispers behind her hand and smiles, and Valentina shakes her head like a Chihuahua getting a bone.

I roll my eyes. Lately, anytime a boy's around they go crazy.

Flashing a big smile, the young man steps in front of the group.

"Welcome! I'm Jaimie Siever, head counselor at Camp Glowing Spring.

And this is my assistant, Trina Long. We're happy to host you guys here this week. It's going to be a blast! You may not want to return to school when it's over."

"You got that right!" blurts out Toby, and Carlos and Nathan laugh. Coach Quackenbush makes a shushing sign with his hands and frowns, and the boys quiet down.

In a tree beside us, a woodpecker taps its beak on a tree. The knocking sound echoes through the woods.

"Look at that, guys!" I try to get Chloe and Valentina's attention.

But they're so busy giving Jaimie goo goo eyes that they don't notice. I guess he is sort of good looking, but he's old enough to shave. Shouldn't they at least have a crush on someone our own age?

"The next few days will be very busy," the head counselor continues, "and you'll have plenty of neat experiences. Make sure to follow all the rules your counselors and activity leaders give, and always have a buddy with you when walking around the camp site. DO NOT wander in the woods by yourself. You can never be sure what you'll find. Now, let's drop your gear off in your cabins and have some fun!"

Kids cheer at the talk about having a good time, but I focus on the second part of Jaimie's speech.

"Why did he warn us not to go in the woods?" I whisper to Mariama.

"They probably don't want us to get lost," she responds. "And I guess it could be dangerous out there after dark."

I almost tell her about the man who looked like Big Foot, but I stop. I don't want her to think I'm as silly as my little brother. Besides, even if Sasquatch was real, he runs away from people. As long as we stick together things will be fine.

After the counselor stops talking, Chloe raises her hand.

"Excuse me, Mr. Siever, are you leading any of our activities?"

"It's Jaimie. And, yeah, I'll be with you at campfire tonight. I also help with some of the water sports and archery."

"Great, Jaimie! I guess we'll see you then." Chloe smiles so big her cheeks might crack.

When he turns to answer a question from a boy in the front row, Valentina giggles and high fives Chloe.

Mariama and I look at each other and shake our heads. This is going to be an interesting retreat.

"Let's line up! Female campers after me!" Jaimie's assistant Trina shouts, and I jump. She may look like a fairy, but she sounds like an army drill sergeant. Her posture is straight like mine is when I walk with a book on my head. And her facial expression is all about business.

"Come on, girls!"

We follow Trina's lead toward a shady area under a large pine. The fresh smell reminds me of our tree last Christmas.

"Once Jaimie gets the boys settled, he'll bring over the room assignment sheet, and I'll take you to your cabins," she says."

While she's talking, a dark shape rises up the road, and I catch my breath. As it moves closer through the trees, I see a flash of white. Realizing it's just another school bus, I relax.

"I thought only our class was coming on the retreat," says Mariama. "Who's that?"

"St. Regis." Valentina reads the name of one of our rival schools on the side of the bus.

Kids hang out the windows and wave.

"Remember when we played St. Regis girls in our last tennis match?" Mariama frowns and turns to Chloe. "Eileen and Cindy were their names. They were really mean."

"Yeah, they cheated and then got mad when we beat them." Chloe put her hands on her hips.

"Well, lucky for us, they won't be in our cabins," I say as the bus turns down a dirt road.

The area under the pine tree gets crowded, as the other sixth grade girls and three counselors join us. There will be four cabins of girls and four cabins of boys.

"It's all yours," Jaimie hands Trina a sheet of paper and moves back to the boys' group. "Let's head to our cabins, guys!"

Trina steps in front of us and calls out names. I cross my fingers that I get to stay with my friends.

"Sophie, Chloe, Valentina, Carly, Christy, Mariama! Follow me to Cabin 3."

CHAPTER SEVEN

Cabin 3

"I call one of the top bunks!" Chloe yells as we step in our cabin.

"Great! Because I want to sleep on the bottom." I set my duffle bag on a bunk near one of the two windows. Trina gives us the cabin rules right after she drops us off.

"Lights out at 12 a.m. sharp each night, and *do not* leave the cabin without a counselor, unless it's an emergency. I need to transport some other girls to their rooms, but I'll be back at 1200 hours to take you to lunch."

"What's 1200 hours?" Valentina asks after Trina steps out.

"It's noon in military time," says Chloe. "My uncle was in the army, and that's how he talks."

"This is nice!" I smile taking in the bright room. Our ride on the worn-out bus up here had me scared our cabin would be a dump. But it's cleaner than I expected, with a shiny, light-colored wood floor, bare wood walls, and a slanted ceiling. There are four bunk beds covered with navy sheets. Cute nylon, drawstring bags with the Camp Glowing Spring logo are left on each one.

The room is air conditioned, thank goodness. Cool air blows from the vent. I'm glad I brought an extra blanket along with my sleeping bag, because I get chilly at night.

"I think I'm gonna like it here!" Christy belts out the lyrics to a song from *Annie* and skips over to another bunk beside mine.

I can see why she was the lead in the school musical last year. She can sing, and she's not shy about talking to anyone. Christy usually hangs around with the artsy kids at school and wears fancy dangling earrings sometimes. Our other bunkmate, Carly Gibson, has a twin brother named Carlton in our class. I don't know her well either, but she seems cool.

"I can't wait to make s'mores tonight!" Valentina does a happy dance in the middle of the floor.

"Yeah, I like mine with double the marshmallows," says Carly. "It'll be neat to be around a real live campfire. They're going to tell us ghost stories and everything."

My chest gets tight. I'm up for the s'mores, but I'm not too sure how I'll like the spooky tales.

"And at bedtime we can play a prank on the boys with this!" Chloe pulls the shaving cream from her bag like a rabbit from a magician's hat.

"Exactly what are you going to do with that shaving cream?" I lean toward the metal can.

"Put it in their sleeping bags. Or we could make mustaches on their faces when they're asleep. Imagine Nathan with one like a handlebar!"

"That will be hilarious!" Valentina cracks up.

"Do you think that's a good idea?" asks Mariama. "What if we get in trouble?"

"We'll only get in trouble if they snitch, and they wouldn't do that," says Chloe. "Kids do pranks at retreat every year. It's tradition."

"We don't even know where their cabin is." I shake my head. "We might get lost."

"Don't be a baby, Sophie," says Valentina. "It'll be fun!"

"Sign me up!" adds Christy. "Pranking the boys will be cool."

My stomach drops like I'm on a roller coaster ride.

Last week I put a plastic roach on Cole's pillow, so I'm definitely no angel. But I don't want to get into any trouble on the retreat. My parents would probably take away my phone until the next school year if they found out. Sneaking out to terrorize the boys isn't worth it. And what if something catches us while we're roaming around at night? Like that hairy man I saw or a wild animal? I've got to think of some way to bow out.

Trina is right on time to take us over for lunch. I'm super excited because my stomach is growling like a grizzly bear.

We trail her like ducklings following a mother duck down the path, and the sunlight reflects off her short blond curls. Trina seems right at home among the leafy trees, thick bushes, and grass, but they make me nervous. You never know what could be hiding in the woods.

"Aaack!" I jump back when I spot something brown and furry to our right.

"Chill, Sophie, it's just a deer," says Christy.

"And she's got a baby with her!" Carly gestures toward the deer's mini-me with excitement.

With large black eyes, pointed ears, and soft looking tan fur, the fawn is its mother's twin. Spooked by our noise and movement, they rustle back through the branches just as quickly as they came out.

"This place is filled with natural wonders," says Trina. "It's great!"

"I love seeing all the animals too," shares Carly. "I want to be a vet one day."

Our tennis shoes and hiking boots crunch through the gravel as we wind along the path. Getting back to the dining hall seems longer than it took to make our way to the cabin. But that may be because I'm starving.

"How long have you worked here?" Chloe quizzes Trina.

"Just this past year," she answers. "I'm studying to be a schoolteacher, and my college gives me credit hours for counseling kids."

"Cool!" says Valentina. "Does Jaimie want to be a teacher too?"

"He works in Camp Glowing Spring's business office, which applies toward his management degree."

"I might want to do something like that when I'm in college, so I won't have to be in class all the time," says Chloe.

"It's a great way to get experience," Trina says as we near a clearing. "Here we are at the mess hall. Think you could find your way back to your cabin, ladies?"

Mariama nods. "I watched for landmarks along the way."

I'm happy someone was paying attention, because I still don't know my way around. I'm not planning on going anywhere by myself during this retreat, so I guess it doesn't matter.

"Great looking out!" says Trina. "See, this trail here? It's a short cut to the boys' cabins and also circles around to where you stay."

The cafeteria is just a few steps ahead, and I smile when I see it. The smoky smell of grilled burgers hits my nostrils as we walk through the door.

"That food looks good!" Mariama exclaims, pointing out the cafeteria options. Besides hamburgers, there's an area with sandwich fixings, a salad bar, and even a make your-own-pancake station, that includes berries, whipped creme, and chocolate. The best part is that it's all you can eat.

"I heard they serve pancakes at every meal!" says Chloe.

"I think it's just breakfast and lunch." Mariama reads an overhead sign.

She and I line up for burgers, and Chloe, Valentina, and Carly walk over to the long line for pancakes.

"Can I hang with you guys?" Christy gets behind us.

"Sure." I move to the side to give her space. I wish we'd gotten here a few minutes earlier, because the place is packed.

Nathan, Toby, and some of the other boys from our school are already chowing down at a table in the center of the room. I don't recognize some of the others at their table.

"This can't just be our group." I look around to figure out what's going on.

"It's those creepy kids from St. Regis!" Mariama whispers, checking out wording on the tee shirts of some boys and girls standing in front of us.

"They must be having their retreat at the same time as we are," says Christy.

"Some of them were mean to Mariama and Chloe at one of our tennis matches," I explain.

"Don't worry about it, Mariama," Christy replies. "They probably won't bother you here."

Someone bumps into us, and Mariama rams into the backside of a girl in front of her.

"Oops! Sorry!" She steps to the side when an Asian girl with a short bob turns around.

It's Eileen, one of the St. Regis tennis players that cheated on Mariama and Chloe.

CHAPTER EIGHT

St. Regis

"No biggie," Eileen says with a blush. "Hey, Cindy! Wait up!"

Not wanting to talk to us, Eileen hops out of the line to join her friends at a nearby table.

Mariama and Christy slide forward to fill in the gap in the line and press into someone else.

"Watch where you're going, clumsy!" A heavy-set boy scowls.

"Who you calling clumsy?" Mariama stands up straight, rolling her neck.

I'm surprised to see her get an attitude, because she's normally the calm one in our group. Her nerves must be rattled from seeing Eileen.

"You, Puff Head, now get out of my space." He narrows his eyes.

"Hey, wait a minute. That's uncalled for." Christy raises her palms. "We didn't bump into you on purpose. You don't have to call people names."

"I'm not calling names," says the boy. "I'm just telling the truth. She's clumsy, and her hair looks like she stuck her finger in a light socket. She needs to brush it."

"That's a good one, Arnold!" A boy beside him with wire rimmed glasses moves forward with a smirk. He's around the same height as his friend, with spiky, reddish-brown hair.

Mariama blinks, and I ball my hands in a fist. I feel like a pot boiling over with hot water.

Mariama's extra-sensitive about her hair since her mom fixes it in African braids and afro puffs. She gets embarrassed when some of the other kids comment on it. Sometimes people ask questions about my tightly curled hair texture too, but since I wear it in longer ponytails that look similar to the way the other girls in our school style their hair, it's not such a big deal.

"Take that back!" Mariama raises her voice and moves closer to Arnold.

"Get away from me, Blackie!" He raises his hand.

Surprised, Mariama jumps back like she hit her finger on a hot stove.

"What did you say?" Christy gets in between them.

"You heard me!" says Arnold. "Mind your own business."

I think of stories my parents tell me and Cole about how they were called names when they were younger because of their skin color.

"Some people are prejudiced against others and don't like them because they come from a different racial group or country," my dad explained.

When he talked about that stuff, I wished he'd be quiet, because it seemed silly. People don't act like that at our school. But now it's actually happening to me.

"You be quiet!" I point my finger at Arnold. "Mariama didn't do anything to you."

"I don't understand jungle talk! Ooo, ooo, ooo!" he says.

"Whoa! Did you hear that?" A tall St. Regis boy with curly, light brown hair taps his friend on the shoulder.

They turn to watch what's happening like they're at the movies. My face is getting warm, and I can feel my heart pounding in my chest. I don't know whether to hit Arnold or run.

"Will you guys go on?" A freckled girl near me complains. "The line is moving. Get your food."

"We're not listening to you jerks anymore." Christy waves her hand at Arnold. "Move."

"Isn't that cute, Brandon?" Arnold presses his fingers beside his eyes and pulls the skin upwards. "The China girl is standing up for her jungle friends! Let's finish getting our lunch before they get germs on it."

They move ahead in the line, and the lady behind the counter hands them their burgers. I hang back a little to stop myself from running up to punch them both. I'm so mad; I'm shaking. Mariama looks like she's about to cry. I feel numb as campers chatter and plates clatter around us.

"Man! You weren't joking when you said those kids from St. Regis were mean, Mariama," says Christy, after we get our cheeseburgers and fries and walk to find a table.

"I can't believe that just happened!" I bite my bottom lip.

"I wish my mom would let me get my hair straightened so it would be smoother." Mariama touches one of her afro puffs.

"Don't say that, Mariama!" I touch her shoulder. "I love your hair. Those boys are racist."

"Yeah, my family's been called plenty of names because we're Asian," says Christy. "Once in the park, somebody told my mom to go back where she came from, and she was born in Houston! She started recording them with her phone and they got scared and ran away. Some people are just dumb bullies. If we see them anymore this week, let's make sure we go the other way."

"I guess that's a good idea," I say. "But I sure would like to get back at them."

Arnold and Brandon disappear after they get their food, thank goodness. I'm ready to sit down.

Finding a place to eat in this place is like working a 1000-piece jigsaw puzzle. Even more seats have been taken since we first came in.

"Sophie, Christy, Mariama!" Chloe calls to us from a rectangular table in the center of the room. Of course, it's right next to Toby and the other boys from our class.

"What's happenin', Captain?" Toby reaches across the table to give me a fist bump when we join them. I'm still a little jittery. Sliding into a chair near my friends feels like coming home.

"We ran into some of the meanest people ever in the lunch line," says Christy.

"Some boys from St. Regis were being just plain racist." I grab a plastic bottle of ketchup to squirt on my fries.

"I couldn't believe all the terrible things they said," Christy agrees.

"What'd they do?" asks Nathan.

"Made fun of my hair and called us names after we accidentally bumped into them," Mariama explains with a shaky voice.

"That's awful!" Carly's face turns red.

"Yeah…that's messed up," Toby says with a frown.

"Cheer up, guys, you probably won't see those jerks the rest of the time we're here," says Chloe. "I heard one of the teachers saying she was happy that there aren't any more combined meals on the schedule. All our activities are with kids from Xavier."

I hope she's right, because fighting with those racists was like being dumped on the head with a bucket of cold water. I'm done with the drama. I'm ready to get back to having fun.

CHAPTER NINE

The Blob

"Where's my beach towel?"

Mom did too good a job of packing my duffle bag. Clothes and towels are rolled up so tightly inside that I can barely find anything.

"Hurry up and change, Sophie." Chloe steps out of the restroom. "Miss Trina will be here to get us in a few minutes."

She looks like a tween model in a red, white, and blue bathing suit and plastic flip flops. I wonder if she bought the outfit special for the retreat. Carly, Mariama, and Christy are also already in their swim gear. Christy rubs sunscreen on Carly's back.

"Don't forget that area between my shoulders, please," says Carly. "I burn really badly there."

When we came back to the cabin after lunch, I took a quick nap, while the other girls played Uno. You'd think I wouldn't be tired since I slept most of the drive up here, but the fight with the St. Regis boys wore me out. We didn't tell Trina, our counselor, what happened. I just want to forget about it. Hopefully, we'll never see them again.

"I'll be done in a sec." I finally find my lime green swimsuit and rush in to the bathroom area to get ready.

My nose wrinkles at the strong Pine-Sol and detergent smell. It's not as nice in here as it is in the main cabin. One side has individual showers covered by white plastic curtains, and the other has bathroom stalls with wooden doors. The walls and ceilings are made of some fake-looking metal material. The gray floor is cement.

"Eek!" I shriek, as a scorpion runs from a back corner under the curtains.

The sight of the two-clawed, bug-like creature makes my skin crawl. *Is it going to come out?*

I wait a second, but don't see or hear anything. I may have to skip taking a shower for the next two days.

Guess I'll change in a bathroom stall. I turn the lever on one of the wooden doors.

Balancing on one foot, I pull off my jeans and attach them to a hook on the back of the door. *Don't want to accidentally step on something.* My mother would be impressed at how fast I change from my clothes into my bathing suit and shove my jeans and tee shirt into my messenger bag. I can't wait to get out of this bathroom.

"I just saw a scorpion in there!" I announce once I rejoin my friends in the cabin.

"Awesome-sauce! You should have called me!" Carly jumps up from her bunk, where she's flipping through a notebook. "Is it still around?"

Carly wasn't joking when she told Trina she's an animal lover. She's even taped a picture of her with her dog, cat, gecko, and pet pig over her twin bed.

"The scorpion ran under the shower curtain," I answer. "I don't know if I want to go back in there for my shower tonight."

"I'm sure it'll be gone by then," says Valentina. "If not, you'll be plenty clean from swimming this afternoon."

"Yeah, a few bounces on the Blob will knock all the dirt off of you!" Mariama says with a laugh.

"I hope one of the bigger boys goes on after me, so I can soar through the clouds!" Chloe holds her arms out like airplane wings.

I want to get on the Blob as much as I want to see Big Foot. I'll give it a try, so I don't look like a baby in front of my friends, but I'm nervous. I was excited when my parents signed the waiver form allowing me to swim on this trip. But after seeing the lake, I wonder if I should have asked to go with the non-swimmers to arts and crafts.

"Trina's here!" yells Chloe. We scramble out the door to meet her. The sun is blinding, and there's not a cloud in the sky. Zero chance of swim time getting canceled due to rain.

The other girls are happy-go-lucky on the way to the lake. I feel like I'm headed to detention. How can they think jumping into water so deep we can't see the bottom of it sounds like fun?

"Last one in is a rotten egg!" Toby yells once we make it to the dock area. He and his friends rush to be the first ones in line for the Blob.

"Awesome-sauce!" exclaims Carly, once we get closer to the lake and the other water activities.

I imagine Big Foot yanking me off the Blob and pulling me down into the deep.

"You guys go on ahead without me," I say, as we catch up to the boys. "I need to use the bathroom."

"Didn't you just go back in the cabin?" asks Mariama.

"I've got to use it again."

"That's fine. I'll wait out here for you," says Chloe, shading her eyes from the sun. This is one time I wish she wasn't such a good friend.

Since I don't really have to do anything in the restroom, I finish up quickly. After I come out, I move like I'm in slow motion as the rest of the sixth graders circle the wooden deck.

"Over here, guys! Come on!" Christy and Carly wave to us.

We're actually going to do this. Though most of the class is in the line, it moves fast. I've got to get myself together soon. I focus on the step planks as we make our way to the top of the deck.

"I'm the king of the world!" Toby lands on his knees and then bounces like a rubber ball into the water, making a giant splash.

"That looks like so much fun!" Chloe taps my shoulder. "We go soon!"

My heart pumps like a locomotive. There's no way to get out of this; we're boxed in.

"I'll jump right after you do, to give you a big bounce." Chloe says.

"Gero-nimo!" Counselor Jamie's voice booms through the air, as he plops on after Miss Trina. Her body flies at least six feet in the air.

Almost our turn. Chloe grabs my hand and I suck air deep into my lungs. About fifteen other people have already gone, and no one has gotten hurt, so I think I can do this. *Oh no, I'm the next one up!*

Mariama slides off the side of the plastic like a fish into the water, just before my turn. I close my eyes and bend my knees.

One. Two. Three. Jump!

"Aaaah!" I scream as I bounce, butt first, on the Blob.

As planned, Chloe thunders down on the plastic as hard as she can behind me. I float through the air like a bird.

"Wheee!"

This is awesome sauce! I can't wait to do it again.

CHAPTER TEN

Ant Attack

My stomach feels fluttery when we walk into the dining hall for dinner. But as Chloe predicted, the St. Regis group is not in the cafeteria with us. The once-bare wood walls are plastered with paintings from the kids who did arts and crafts while we were at the lake. Our classmates who are already eating laugh and talk excitedly with their friends.

"Where are the burgers and pizza?" Carly frowns after we step up to the serving area.

Chicken, rice, green beans, and wheat rolls are our only option, unless we want to get something from the salad bar.

"It looks pretty good," says Mariama. "I guess they want to make sure we eat some veggies while we're here."

I nod in agreement and grab my tray. Green beans are one of the few vegetables I like.

"There's Toby!" exclaims Chloe. She, Christy, and Valentina make a bee line for the boys' table after we've all been served.

"It's too crowded over there." I turn to Mariama and Carly. "Let's take this seat near the window."

You'd think the sixth graders would be tired out from all our earlier activities, but the room is as charged as a cell phone on 100 percent.

"Watch out!" To our left, Carly's twin brother, Carlton squirts silly string at his friends. We laugh and cover our plates with our hands until he settles down.

After about 30 minutes, Trina and the counselors stand up with signs with our cabin numbers on them. We clear off our tables and join them to go back to our cabins to rest a bit before campfire time.

Back in the room, we lounge on our bunks. Chloe and Valentina giggle at their favorite boy band stars in teen magazines.

"Did you notice how cute Jaimie looked in his swim trunks earlier?" Chloe asks. "His muscles are huge."

"Yes, and I also saw how much time he was spending with Trina," Mariama looks up from a notebook she's writing in. "I think they like each other."

"How could he like her?" Chloe frowns. "She acts like an army captain."

"I don't know, but they jumped on the Blob together almost every time." Carly leans her head down from the top bunk. "Plus, they're both in college."

Chloe pokes her lip out and pulls threads on her throw blanket. Noticing that my best friend is getting upset, I change the subject.

"Can you believe it, guys? Christy has never had s'mores before!"

"Never had s'mores?" Chloe perks up. "Girl, you are missing out!"

"We don't eat too many sweets around our house," Christy explains. "My mom mostly gets nuts and dried fruits for snacks."

"At our house we eat beans and rice all the time." Valentina nods her head in understanding. "The only time I eat foods from different cultures is at school or sleepovers. I really don't mind, though, because my grandma's tamales are delicioso!"

"Tell me about it!" I rub my belly. "And her churros are sooo good! Speaking of which, do you have any churros left over from this morning?"

"Si, amiga, there are a few in my bag." She reaches in the corner beside her bunk then jumps back like she's gotten shocked.

"Ahhhh!"

"What is it!" Chloe looks up.

"Ants!" screams Valentina.

I lean over her shoulder, and the hair on the back of my neck stands up. Hundreds of tiny black bugs crawl all over the dropped churros. They must have gotten in from cracks by the wall and the ceiling. Though the sight makes my skin crawl, I can't seem to look away.

Valentina is freaking out. "Help me clean this up!" She jumps up and down to get scattering bugs off her sneakers.

"Here, use this." Carly hands us some wet paper towels she just got from the restroom. "We probably shouldn't have food in here."

Still shrieking, Valentina drops a sopping napkin over the brown paper bag and then plops it in the trash.

"Disgusting!"

Though we aren't acting as crazy as Valentina, the other girls and I move back. But Carly is as cool as a cucumber.

"Those little guys were having a feast. After we clean the rest of this up, set the trash can outside."

Valentina squirts sanitizer in the area to make sure there are no ants left.

"How are you so good at dealing with bugs and animals?" I ask when Carly and I are in the restroom washing our hands.

"I dunno." She shrugs her shoulders. "I've always liked working with living things."

"That's cool that you already know you want to be a veterinarian when you grow up. I have no clue what job I want to do right now."

"It's my passion," she says. "I guess I am lucky to have figured it out so early. My brother Carlton likes animals too, but he doesn't want to be a vet."

"Gracias for cleaning up that mess!" Valentina hugs us both after we come back into the room. "I thought I might faint."

"It's a good thing we noticed it before we were getting ready for bed," says Mariama.

"Yeah, that would have been a nightmare!" says Chloe with a giggle. "Speaking of bedtime…anybody got any ideas on when we should prank the boys?"

Not that again. I grit my teeth. *Haven't we had enough excitement today?* Once we get back from the campfire I was looking forward to snuggling up in my bunk. The last thing I want to do is risk getting lost in the woods for a prank.

"Does anyone even know where the boys' cabins are?" I ask.

"I saw them on the way to lunch this afternoon," says Mariama. "There's a turnoff just before you enter that clearing by the dining hall."

"Will we be able to see that trail at night? What if we get lost?"

"Somebody sounds like they are chickening out." Chloe puts her hand on my arm. "Relax, Sophie, it'll be fun."

"She's making a good point," says Christy. "I don't know the place Mariama is talking about either. Let's check it out on the way to the campfire, and if we don't see it, we can do the prank tomorrow."

"That sounds like a plan," Chloe says to my relief.

I'm happy I'm not the only one not in favor of wandering around in the woods after dark. If it seems too scary, maybe Christy will stay in the cabin with me.

Knock! Knock! Knock!

There are three quick raps on the door, and Trina steps in.

"Wow! You look pretty," exclaims Christy.

Trina's skin is tan from our time out on the lake earlier, and her lips shine with a pink gloss. Some kind of shadow is on her eyes that make them seem bigger and bluer. She's dressed up her jeans and Camp Glowing Spring Tee Shirt with a bright red flower behind her ear.

"Thanks so much, Christy!" She blushes. "I decided to get a bit festive for the campfire tonight."

"Is it a special occasion?" Chloe puts her hands on her hips and frowns.

"No, just the usual," says Trina, "but since I live out here for an entire school semester, I sometimes want a change. Of course, it will be definitely be a neat experience for you guys, since it's your class retreat. S'mores and a campfire are wonderful anytime."

"I've been waiting for this since we got here!" Valentina pumps her fist in the air. "I love s'mores, and sitting by a real campfire sounds so cool."

"Alright, let's get moving, ladies!" Trina shifts back to counselor mode. "Grab your bug spray and some water. They expect us to meet the group at 2200 hours! Onward and upward!"

CHAPTER ELEVEN

S'Mores

On the way out, Chloe whispers that 2200 means 10 p.m. Trina really knows about the military. I hope she's also had survival training; we might need it out here.

It's pitch black on the trail. You need x-ray vision to clearly see. No way am I pranking the boys' cabin tonight.

I'm glad Trina reminded us to put on bug spray because the warm air is thick with mosquitoes. They'd suck the s'mores out of us if we didn't have our insect repellent on to keep them away.

Though we can barely see anything, I'm surprised at how noisy the forest is after dark. Crickets chirp, frogs croak, and birds tweet, every few minutes. If I had to sleep outside, I'd need my ear plugs to get any rest.

"This way, girls." It feels like we're playing blind man's bluff as Trina leads us along the path.

None of us talks much because we're concentrating on staying with the group.

"Sorry!" I stumble on a fallen branch and hold onto Chloe's arm to keep from falling.

"Here, this way." She guides me back to the path.

We make it to a clearing, and the full moon cuts through the blackness. Thoughts of Big Foot dance around my mind like the large tree shadows. Suddenly, I remember Cole's warning:

Big Foot lives in the woods and is nocturnal, so that means he comes out at night.

I shiver. This is the monster's favorite time of day.

"Over there, y'all!" Carly's voice rings out, and I flinch.

An owl stares at us from a low branch on a pine tree. Its yellow eyes and white feathers shine like glow sticks. It's as still as a statue, and for a second, I wonder if it's real. Then slowly, it turns its head around to the back of its neck like a wind-up doll.

"That. Is. Spooky!" Valentina cries. "Man, I wish I had my camera."

"I read somewhere that owls can rotate their heads 270 degrees," says Carly. "Must be why they are such great hunters."

"Hunters?!" exclaims Chloe. "What do owls eat?"

"Small things, like mice, frogs, lizards, sometimes rabbits...."

"I'm glad they don't have an appetite for people, or we'd be in trouble," I say, and twist my neck around to see how far it can go.

"Get a move on, ladies! We're almost there." Trina waves us on.

We hustle to catch up to her and Christy. When I see brightness ahead, I quicken my steps.

"There's the fire!" Christy shouts.

The pit is humongous. Flames lick the sky. The smell of burning wood makes my nose itch.

It feels warm near the campfire, like a sunny day on the beach. A few trees were probably cut to make the logs. Fist-sized, round rocks surround the crackling blaze. Our group gathers around like a family reunion. Their darkened bodies against the flames remind me of silhouettes I traced in kindergarten. I strain my eyes to see if I recognize any of our other friends.

"There's Nathan, Toby, and Carlos!" Chloe points out our classmates, who are shoving marshmallows onto narrow sticks.

She also spots Jaimie, the counselor, standing off to the side, and her face breaks into a goofy grin. When Trina leaves us and walks over to Jaimie, Chloe's frown turns upside down. The counselors laugh like they are telling an inside joke, and then Jaimie hands Trina a medium-sized, square box.

"What did I tell you?" Mariama tilts her head in their direction. "Jaimie and Trina like each other! I'll bet that's why she's all dressed up."

Chloe looks their way like a kid who didn't get invited to a birthday party. This is really getting old. She doesn't even know Jaimie, and he's almost old enough to be her dad. I wish she didn't get so wound up over boys all the time.

Trina walks back over to us and points to an empty space in the circle. "Take a seat there, guys. Here's your gear for s'mores." She sets the box on the ground nearby.

"Now how do we make this again?" Christy stares into the box full of s'more's ingredients like it's a treasure chest.

"It's just like fixing a sandwich, easy-peasy," says Mariama. "Heat a marshmallow on one of the sticks, then put it and a piece of chocolate between two graham crackers and eat."

"I like to put mine back in the fire with tongs after I put the top piece of graham cracker on," says Carly. "It makes it extra toasty."

"Look how fat my marshmallow's getting!" Valentina's eyes widen as the marshmallow on her stick starts to melt.

"Don't leave it in too long, or it'll burn," warns Trina.

"Mmm…this is ooey, gooey good!" Christy gives the thumbs up after she takes her first bite.

"Now you're not a s'mores newbie anymore!" Chloe laughs from across the flames.

I eat so many s'mores my tummy is tight as a drum. The warm fire feels great. After everyone's finished eating the counselors lead us in two campfire songs. When we finish, Jaimie grabs Trina's hand and squeezes it, and she looks at the ground with a shy smile.

I'm sure I won't have nightmares about Big Foot back in our cabin because I'm so tired my head's already drooping. Chloe lays her head on Valentina's shoulder, so they must be getting sleepy too.

Ding! Ding! Ding!

The sharp sound of a fork hitting a tin can knocks off that cozy feeling. After getting our attention, Jaimie stands up.

"It's almost time to head back to your cabins for lights-out. But before we go, I want to share another Camp Glowing Spring tradition. For decades, kids just like you have sat around this campfire, enjoying s'mores, singing songs…and hearing the Legend of the Ghost of Camp Glowing Spring."

The legend of what!? My eyes pop open. My heart starts racing like I've been running laps around the tennis court. Nobody told us there was a ghost around here. What's this all about?

CHAPTER TWELVE

The Ghost of Camp Glowing Spring

"Awesome-sauce!" Carly scoots in closer to the circle. "I love scary stories. Bring it on!"

This is about the fifth time on this trip that I wish I had my ear plugs. The last thing I want to hear before bedtime is a legend about a ghost.

It's nearly black again in the woods, since the fire has died down some. The trees surround us like giants. I wrap my arms around my shoulders as Jaimie begins.

"On an evening like tonight a boy about your age went missing. The rangers said his name was Jessie, and he was on a school retreat, just like you guys. That first night around the campfire, the counselors warned the campers to stick together. Jessie ignored them, wandering off into the woods when everyone was eating s'mores. He had a pet snake collection at home and thought he might find a cool one in the forest to add to it."

"Sit down, Toby!" Chloe yells across the fire with a giggle as he pretends to tiptoe away from the group. Carlos, Nathan, and some of the other boys elbow each other and laugh. Somebody swings a rubber snake in the air.

"That's enough, guys," calls Coach Quackenbush.

Jaimie holds up his hands to settle the kids back down and continues with the story.

"When the campers lined up to go to the cabins for the night, Jessie's friends noticed he was missing. The other kids were taken to their bunks, and the lead counselor and some chaperones went out with flashlights to look for him. 'Jes-sie! Jes-sie! Jeeees-ie!' they called."

"Come home, Jessie!" Nathan screams, and the boys start laughing again.

Our fire has died down, and I huddle closer to Christy and Carly. The stars light the sky like diamonds. The cooler breeze gives me goosebumps. Not scared, Chloe, Valentina, and Mariama shake with laughter at the boys' antics.

"Suddenly, a thunderstorm blew in," says Jaimie. "Sheets of rain fell, making it hard for the search party to see. The chaperones decided to go back to the cabins, where their own kids were, and continue looking for Jessie when the storm ended. The lead counselor felt responsible and stayed in the woods to look a little longer.

"Jessie, meanwhile, made it back to the cabins before the rest of the group. As soon as he saw lightning, he'd gotten scared and headed back. Jessie had a few mosquito bites and scratches but was otherwise in good shape. He was sad he didn't find the snake he was looking for.

"It turned out to be one of the worst thunderstorms the area had ever seen. The lead counselor did not come home that night or the next morning. By lunchtime, a search party was sent out. The chaperones and the area police searched high and low for days. But the counselor disappeared without a trace, never to be heard from again."

"That was over ten years ago, but some say on dark nights you can still hear the counselor's ghost calling for the lost boy. Listen, you can hear it now, Jes-sie! Jes-sie...."

"JESSIE!" calls a voice from across the woods.

A flashlight flickers, and the extremely tall, scraggly-haired man in a baggy jacket and pants that I saw earlier rises out of the shadows.

"Ahhhh!" My friends and I and half the other kids shriek.

As quickly as the light flashed on, it's off, and the man vanishes. Jaimie runs down the path he came from.

With the head counselor out of sight, Coach Quackenbush moves to the empty space in front of the group.

"Er, alright, ladies and gents, it's time to head back to your cabins for some shut eye. Let's thank your counselors for that exciting story." He claps his hands, and we join in.

"Woot! Woot! Woot!" cheer the boys.

A few seconds later, Jaimie eases back and whispers something to Trina, off to the side. When Coach Quackenbush finishes talking, the two counselors say something to him.

"Where did that man go?" asks Valentina. "What's going on?"

I glance around to see if I can see him.

"I dunno." Carly rubs her arms. "I think he ran back in the woods."

I squint over to the area where the man stood again. It's too dark to see if he left footprints.

"You call this scary?!" calls out Toby. "Give me a break."

"Yeah, that was fake, man," agrees Carlos. "That was probably one of the counselors. There's no ghost out here."

But what if it wasn't a ghost? I think about how hairy he seemed. And how up close, he was definitely even taller than my dad.

"That man looked like Big Foot!" I whisper to my friends.

"Come on, Sophie, you know that's not real." Chloe pats my back.

"Cole and I saw a show about Big Foot the other day, and I didn't believe it." I shift my eyes around the woods. "But that man we saw looked just like the creature that was on TV. I think I saw him earlier right after we got here too."

"Let's get back to the cabin, girls." Trina pops up beside us like a genie, interrupting the conversation.

"Did you see that man, Trina? Who was he?" I ask.

"Jaimie's always adding things to these campfire stories to make them more thrilling." She shrugs her shoulders. "Who knows? I'm not part of that committee. Okay, let's get a move on! We want lights out at 2345 hours."

"I wish she'd just say near midnight." Chloe yawns. "Figuring out this military stuff this late at night makes my head hurt."

We follow Trina like soldiers along the dark path.

"You guys aren't worried about that man we just saw?" I ask my friends.

"I'm with the boys," says Mariama. "That was probably somebody the camp counselors hired to scare us."

"It was just a spooky story for fun, Soph." Chloe wraps her arm around my shoulders. "You heard Trina. Jaimie and the counselors made all this up. Big Foot and ghosts don't exist."

I hope they're right.

"Jaimie's a fantastico actor," says Valentina. "I wonder if he does plays in college?"

"Didn't he look cute up there?" Chloe sighs.

"Jes-sie! Jes-sie!" Toby and Carlos shriek as we get closer to our cabins.

With each of their howls, my heart thunks in my chest. I can't wait to be safe in my bunk.

My friends and the counselors act like this is a joke. But that man at the campfire looked too close to the monster Cole and I saw on television. And what about the man I saw earlier? Before tonight, I thought Big Foot was just as silly as everyone else does. Now I'm not so sure.

CHAPTER THIRTEEN

The Letter

Tweet. Snort. Tweet. My eyes open to birds singing and Chloe's freight-train-level snores. Her breathing is so loud I'm surprised the bed isn't shaking. I guess she was really tired last night too.

"Buenas dias, Sophie!" Valentina looks up from a journal she's writing in. "I hope you slept well."

"I did." I yawn and stretch my arms over my head. "What time is it?"

"Nearly time for breakfast." Christy steps out of the restroom with Carly and Mariama. "You and Chloe need to get moving, so we're not late."

"Wakey, wakey, eggs and bakey!" I pull on Chloe's foot that's hanging off the edge of the bunk bed.

"I hear you. Here I come," she says in her scratchy, morning voice. She yanks the covers away from her eyes to rouse herself, and then slips off the bed like a preschooler on a playground slide.

Still sleepy, we walk into the bathroom together. The air feels warm and damp from the shower running this morning. I'm glad I took mine after we came back from swimming yesterday. I'm not taking any chances of seeing that scorpion a second time. I want to finish in here fast.

"Jaimie sure did look great last night, didn't he?" Chloe asks while I brush my teeth.

I grunt and shake my head. Luckily, I still have sleepy stuff in my lashes so she can't see me giving her the side eye. I hope I never get as ditsy as Chloe is over boys. Even I can tell that Jaimie likes Trina, someone his own age. Chloe should give it a rest. My best friend is still looking in the mirror after I wash my face, dress, and head back into the main cabin.

"Trina dropped this off for you on her way to go running." Carly throws an envelope on my bunk while I shove my pajamas back in my bag. It's a letter from Cole!

"My brother must have mailed this before I left from home!" I say out loud, scanning his boxy handwriting. The little guy gets on my nerves a lot of the time, but he always knows how to make me smile.

I admire the stamp with a picture of famous Black hair product inventor Madame C.J. Walker on the top right-hand corner of the envelope. According to one of Cole's books, she was the first female, self-made millionaire and lived in the late 1800s and early 1900s. Madame C.J. Walker made all her money selling beauty products to Black women. I wonder if the St. Regis boys who teased me and Mariama about our hair and skin have heard of her.

I break the envelope seal and pull out two light blue sheets of paper. The first one is a note and, underneath, is a drawing of a hairy, ape man.

Dear Sophie,

You are probably in your second day of camp now. I hope you are having fun. I'll miss you, even though Mom and Dad promised that we'd get pizza for dinner while you are away. What's camp like? Is your cabin made of logs? It must be fun to sleep in a real bunk bed.

Please be careful out in the woods! I learned more about Big Foot that may keep you safe:

1. He likes to eat apples.

2. He has psychic powers. (That means he can read your mind.)

3. He has glowing green eyes.

I have to get ready for bed now, so I have to go. I can't wait until you come home!

Love Your Little Brother,
Cole

P.S. If you do see Big Foot try to take a picture!

I guess no one told Cole that we had to turn in our cell phones. If I run into that scary man from last night again, he'd get a kick out of seeing a photo. I'll make sure to show Cole's Big Foot drawing to our art teacher when we go back to school. My brother has won ribbons in a few art contests. I wish I had his talent. The best I can do is stick figures.

"Lucky! You've already got mail!" Finally, out of the bathroom Chloe glances over my shoulder. "Is it from a boy?"

"Just a letter from Cole." I fold the papers back into the envelope.

"Wow! He missed you before you even left home." She holds a hand mirror close to her face.

"Yeah, I miss him too," I answer.

Yesterday, I was happy to leave Cole and my parents, but it *would* be neat if he could enjoy some of the fun things at camp. I'm sure he'd have a blast on the Blob and making s'mores too. I'll tell him everything he has to look forward to at the sixth-grade class retreat when I get home.

"Everybody almost ready?" calls Mariama. "Trina said she'd pick us up at 8:30 a.m. sharp."

"What's that on your face, Chloe?" Valentina stares at her lips.

"Oh, just a little lip gloss." She turns her cheek to the side.

"What's the point of putting on makeup when we're eating breakfast and then hiking in the woods?" asks Mariama. "It'll just wear off."

"Yeah, and when did you start using that stuff?" I ask.

"Can you feel the love tonight!" Christy sashays across the floor singing a song from the musical *The Lion King*.

"Shut up, silly!" Chloe picks up a pillow and throws it at her. "It's not night, it's daytime, and I am *not* in love! There's nothing wrong with wanting to look your best."

What's silly is putting a bunch of glop on your face for a boy who doesn't know you exist, I think. But I don't say anything.

"Ready, ladies?!" Trina pops her head in the doorway. "Time for breakfast! Don't forget your drawstring bags, bug spray, and sunscreen because we're taking a hike after."

"Yes! I'm starving," says Carly. "I want to eat at the pancake buffet again this morning."

"They were delish! You need to try some too, Sophie," Chloe grabs my arms. "Let's get going. It's going to be a great day!"

CHAPTER FOURTEEN

Scavenger Hunt

"Who's ready to explore the trail?" Trina waves our group towards her outside the cafeteria door after breakfast.

We skip behind her along the path. It's so beautiful out here it looks fake. Squint-your-eyes bright sunshine and clear skies perfectly contrast the green grass and trees. Chloe waves at Toby, Nathan, and Carlos as they break off into another small group with Jaimie and three other boys. We gather to listen to Trina under a shady pine.

"You're in for a real treat this morning!" she continues. "We're doing a scavenger hunt. On our two-mile hike you'll see much of Camp Glowing Springs's amazing plant and wildlife. Check off what we see on these sheets I'm handing out. I've got extra water bottles in my pack for each of you. Put them in your bags."

"Awesome-sauce! I love hiking!" Carly slides a visor on over her shoulder-length blond hair. "Maybe we'll see some more animals!"

"That owl's head-turn the other day was fantasti-co," agrees Valentina.

If you ask me, this hike should be optional. I got my fill of the woods last night. What if we run into that scary, hairy-looking man again? How will we escape?

Chloe passes me my water bottle and the scavenger hunt list, and I scan the twenty or so items on it. Acorn, pinecone, moss, mushrooms, rocks…we could find all those things near our cabin. Why chance getting lost in the woods?

Wait a minute, what's the last thing on the sheet? Animal tracks? I shudder. I don't want to get anywhere near anything big enough to leave footprints.

We line up to begin walking, and I ball my hands into fists. I'm happy that other small groups from our retreat are behind us.

"Watch your steps, ladies," warns Trina. "Some of these rocks and branches make the path uneven."

I remember how I almost tripped yesterday and tread carefully. As we get further along the trail and the trees and tall grasses get thicker, I hold my breath. My friends chatter like we're in the hallway at Xavier.

It starts smelling like someone squirted a bottle of perfume, and then I notice a bush, filled with white, bell-shaped flowers.

"What are those?" Mariama asks out loud.

"Honeysuckle," answers Trina. "My mother used to keep them in our yard when I was growing up. They are actually pretty tasty."

"You ate a flower?" I raise my brow.

"The nectar is delicious." Trina nods her head. "But the berries on those bushes are poisonous."

Everyone seems to have forgotten about Big Foot, so I don't mention him. But I keep my eyes peeled. I should grab some poisonous honeysuckle berries to use on an attacker if we need them.

As we continue on the hike, I relax. Things aren't so spooky in the forest when the sun's out as they seemed last night. Bony witch fingers turn back into bumpy tree branches, and slithering snakes become plain old vines.

"There's a squirrel, guys!" Christy pulls out a stubby pencil to mark the animal off her list. "And it's got an acorn; that's on our sheet too."

Frozen for a second, the rodent boldly picks up the round nut it dropped and scurries up an oak tree.

"Good looking out, Christy!" Chloe gives her a high five. "I want to check off everything on my sheet."

"There's some mushrooms!" exclaims Mariama. "And a pine cone!"

"I see a flowering tree over there!" I point out a crepe myrtle with dark, pink blossoms.

"You guys are going to have this thing filled out before we make it halfway on our hike." Trina looks back and smiles.

A few of the other things on the list are harder to find.

"Lizards are everywhere in Houston," says Chloe. "But I haven't spotted one here."

"Be patient," Carly advises. "Sometimes animals get shy with so many people around."

"Can we count the deer that we saw when we got here?" Mariama looks at the items on the list.

"It needs to be things that we see out here on the trail," says Trina.

We move along for ten more minutes without seeing anything. Sweet birdsong makes soft background music. I lift my face to the sun and breathe in the fresh air.

As the path gets steeper my calves tighten, and I rub them. Though the trees keep it shady, the air is still warm out here. I wipe my sweaty forehead with the back of my hand.

"Lions, and tigers and bears, oh my!" Toby, Carlos, Nathan and some other kids chant a few yards behind us.

"Let's calculate how many steps it takes to get back to the cabin," calls Nathan.

"Dude, you're such a dork!" answers Toby. "I'm surprised you didn't bring your math book out here."

"I wish those goofballs would be quiet!" says Carly. "They're scaring the wildlife away."

She's really serious about this scavenger hunt. But I'm happy to hear other people nearby. If we're lucky, they'll frighten Big Foot or anything dangerous away.

The boys' out-of-tune voices follow us as we tramp up the path.

"It's a wonder you don't go back and sing with them," I joke to Christy.

"If they start *Somewhere Over the Rainbow*, I just might," she says and laughs.

"Up ahead, guys! Check that out!" Mariama nods at what looks like a fluffy cotton ball in the ground.

"It's a rabbit!" exclaims Chloe. "See, that's his hole."

We get closer, and the gray and white bunny wiggles its backside. Once its full body makes it to daylight, the rabbit twitches its nose and scampers off into the grass.

I'm just as giddy as the other girls as I check it off my paper. "That was so cute!"

"We may get this scavenger hunt sheet completed yet!" Trina throws her fist in the air to signal us forward.

Our next stop is near a small stream. I know we're getting close when my nose fills with the smell of wet dirt and pine needles. We step off the path to get a closer look at the winding waters.

"If you ever come out here to camp for a longer period, you'll get a chance to fish in our streams and lakes," says Trina. "There are some delicious trout and bass in these waters."

"There's some moss!" Mariama examines the fuzzy green coating on the water-covered rocks.

"We only have three things left to find!" Chloe double checks her list. "A deer, a lizard, and animal tracks."

I'm about ready for this nature hike to end. Lizards seem slimy, and I doubt we'll see another deer. Any animal with prints big enough for us to notice is also big enough to bite someone.

"Lizard alert!" Carly points out a small reptile crawling close to my shoe. "It reminds me of a tiny dinosaur!"

More like a baby Godzilla. I step away from the reptile and walk back toward the path while the others continue to explore.

Suddenly, a large indent on the ground catches my eye. Chloe comes up behind me as I bend down to get a closer look.

"Hey Sophie, what'cha looking at?"

A giant footprint.

CHAPTER FIFTEEN

Into the Woods

My body feels as cold as an ice pop as we stare at the large, muddy tracks. They're the biggest footprints I've ever seen.

"It that from a bear?" Chloe wonders.

I'm not sure, but I don't want to stick around to find out.

"Trina! Guys!" I call. "Look what we found."

"What do we have here?" Carly points at the impressions with a thick stick she's just picked up.

"I'm not sure," Trina frowns. "These tracks are similar to those of a large animal, but see this area in the back of the print that looks like a heel? It makes them seem almost human."

It's hard to tell where the footprints are headed. Some scatter around in this area, others wind down a side trail back into the woods.

"Is it safe for us to be out here?" I ask. "Maybe we should go back to our cabins."

"The tracks aren't fresh." Trina shakes her head. "The water has washed most of them away. It's doubtful that whatever made this is still around. I haven't heard of there being bears in the area, but you never know. I'll alert the park ranger when we return to camp headquarters. We've reached the end of the trail, so it's time to head back anyway. Ladies, this way!"

She leads us to the path the footprints followed. I'm happy we're getting out of here. The short trail leads us back to the cabins without passing the other small groups of campers. It's cool how Camp Glowing Spring is set up to allow for private scavenger hunts. It's like a maze. And it's the perfect place for a creature like Sasquatch to hide.

"Cole would have loved seeing those tracks," I tell Chloe as we move back along the path.

"He probably would've thought it was Big Foot," she laughs.

I'm starting to agree with my little brother. Those prints were too big to come from a bear. Trina says they weren't made today. But that mysterious "man" who came to our campfire in the woods could have run back here last night, couldn't he?

Since this trail is close to the stream it's damp. After a few minutes of walking, the bottoms of my sneakers are caked with mud.

"I may have to dip these in the lake when we get back." I lift up one of my feet to show my dirty shoe.

"I'm with you," says Chloe. "I wish I'd brought some of my older tennis shoes instead of my new ones."

"Let me put this scavenger hunt sheet back in my bag before I drop it." I pull on the baby blue drawstring.

"You guys aren't giving up on looking are you?" Carly calls back to us. "We still haven't spotted a deer yet. Keep watching the bushes."

I shrug my shoulders but keep the paper in my hand, so she'll be happy. What's the big deal? It's not like we're winning a prize for the scavenger hunt. When it comes to nature, Carly is hard core.

I just want to get back to our cabin to safety. That hairy man could still be out here. Plus, it's getting uncomfortable. The pathway is narrower on this trail than the one we used on the way up, and there are way more bugs.

"I can barely see!" Mariama swats gnats out of her face. "I wish I brought sunglasses."

"It's a good thing we didn't wear shorts, or our legs would be covered in bites," Christy agrees.

"Just a few more yards ahead and we'll reach another clearing." Trina waves us forward. "The path gets wider there, and there are fewer insects."

"I think I see a deer to the right!" shrieks Carly. "Look."

We stop for a second while she pokes her stick toward something brown in the brush. We're all disappointed to see that it's just a piece of dark fabric hanging from the trees, and not Bambi.

"That probably ripped off a hiker's jacket or something," says Trina, as we continue to move along.

I skip down the path with the others to make it from the narrow trail to a more comfortable spot. Though I'm antsy about the chance of running into Big Foot, overall, I did enjoy the scavenger hunt and the hike. The woods are very pretty, and I've never seen a real-live rabbit outside a pet store.

"Check out that cardinal!" Carly nods at a scarlet bird with a black face and red beak on a tree branch to our left. "That bird in the nest across from him is a robin."

The robin tilts its head to the side like it understands our conversation. Not as bright as the cardinal, with a dark, gray coat, reddish-orange colored breast and a tangerine beak, it's still just as beautiful.

"I believe that's a female robin," says Trina. "Some say male robins have brighter colored breasts to attract their attention."

"That's so cool," says Valentina. "I never paid so much attention to birds until this trip."

"Me either," says Christy. "When I get home, I'm asking my mom if we can get a bird feeder so more will come to our yard."

"I feel like I've accomplished my goal today." Trina turns around with a smile. "Getting you kids more attuned to nature is one of Camp Glowing Springs's aims. There is so much to see in the great outdoors if we just open our eyes."

A few minutes later, we're back in the clearing near the cafeteria. Our scavenger hunt and nature hike is complete.

"You girls head to your cabin and freshen up a bit," says Trina. "I'll be back to pick you up for your next activity at 1100 hours. Jaimie is the leader, and you'll be grouped with some of the boys' cabins."

Chloe and Valentina pantomime a victory cheer.

"What will we be doing?" I ask.

"Archery."

CHAPTER SIXTEEN

Peanut Butter

"I've always wanted to learn to shoot a bow and arrow!" Christy claps her hands. "My theater group did a *Robin Hood* play last year and had archery props with our costumes. This is going to be super cool!"

The only thing I know about archery is that it's used in the movie *The Hunger Games*. Mom and Dad won't let us watch it for family movie night because they say it's violent and might give Cole nightmares. I may check the book out from our school library after we get back home.

"I hope nobody gets hurt," says Mariama, looking at pictures of Camp Glowing Springs's archery area on a brochure.

"The bows they use at camp are made of plastic, so they aren't really dangerous." Carly replies as she pulls off her hiking boots and wiggles her toes. Before we came in, Chloe, Valentina, and I set our muddy shoes to dry by a nearby tree in the sun.

Trina dropped us off at our cabin for a thirty-minute rest, or siesta, as Valentina calls it, before she comes to take us to the archery range. I'm glad for the break. We went nonstop yesterday, and this morning's hour-long hike wore me out.

"How does this look?" Chloe flutters some fake eyelashes she's glued on. She's sitting on Valentina's bunk, which is beside mine, while Valentina changes in the restroom.

"Like you've got caterpillars over your eyes." I say with a laugh. "Why do you keep getting made up when we're just relaxing at camp?"

"Jaimie and the boys will be in our group, and I want to be ready."

"For what?" I shrug my shoulders. "Seems to me that all that extra hair over your eyes will make it harder to see the target."

Chloe ignores me and turns back to her hand mirror to adjust the lashes. Valentina comes out and plops beside her on the bunk.

"This could be the start of something new. It feels so right to be here with you...." Christy starts singing from another musical again. "I think it's exciting that Chloe is on her way to finding true love!" She places one hand over the other one across her heart.

"You are so dramatic, Christy!" laughs Valentina. "But I agree with you. I'm happy my friend has met the man of her dreams."

I pull out a comic book to look at and ignore them. If you ask me, Chloe's relationship with Jaimie is about as real as they think Big Foot is. She's barely even spoken to him.

Someone knocks on the door, and it opens.

"Ready, guys?" Trina shows up just in time.

She's still wearing the hiking gear she had on earlier, but her cheeks are rosy, and her lips look like she put on a little of the gloss she had on last night.

"Are you going to do archery with us too?" asks Chloe. "I thought we were having another leader."

"Jaimie asked me to stick around to help, so I'll be there, but he'll be the one leading your instruction," Trina answers.

I set my comic book down and hop off the bed. I'm curious to see what doing archery will be like. I surprised myself by enjoying the nature walk, so this may be fun too. The other girls must be just excited to try out archery as I am, because all five of them beat me out the door.

Chloe gathers her sneakers up from under the tree and squats down to put them on.

"Ewww! What's this?"

She yanks her foot out of her tennis shoe, right after she puts it in. "There's something squishy in here!"

The bottom of her foot has a light brown, creamy paste on it.

"Gross!" I step back.

"It's peanut butter!" Chloe sniffs and snatches off her sock.

The other girls start laughing.

I pick up my shoes to see if they have peanut butter in them too. A thick glob is spread butter knife smooth in both of them.

"My shoes are ruined!" Valentina holds her sneakers upside down. "Abuela is going to be so mad."

"Looks like someone has been playing pranks," Trina scans the area. "We don't encourage it because sometimes they get out of hand, but it happens on many of our retreats."

"The prankster must have finished out his lunch out here too." She kicks three browned apple cores. They remind me of something, but I don't know what.

"These are the only sneakers I brought. What am I going to wear now?" Chloe cries.

"Did you girls bring shower shoes?" asks Trina. We nod yes.

"Go get those, and I'll take your tennis shoes to housekeeping to wash while you do archery." She pulls a plastic grocery bag out of her backpack, and we drop our sneakers and Chloe's socks inside.

"Oh, and Chloe…" Trina looks at her eyes and frowns, and then shakes her head. "Never mind."

For a second, I thought she was going to say something about her false eyelashes.

Chloe, Valentina, and I rush back into the cabin to change our footwear.

"That settles it!" Chloe slides into sparkly, plastic flip flops. "We're definitely pranking Toby and Carlos tonight."

"Si, amiga! This is war," says Valentina. "Those boys have some nerve."

"We don't know if it was them who put the peanut butter in our shoes." I root through my bag and see another pair of sneakers.

"Well, I'm sure it was." Chloe tosses her curls. "And I'm getting payback. I wish I'd pranked them with the shaving cream last night."

The rest of the group is already heading up the trail when we come out, and we jog to catch up. Trina is serious about keeping to her time schedule.

On the way to the activity, Chloe and Valentina whisper their plans to prank the boys tonight. I hope I can figure out a good excuse to bail. With that wild man from last night on the loose there's no way I want to wander around the woods after dark.

CHAPTER SEVENTEEN

Cupid's Arrow

Archery is going strong when we get to the wide, grassy field. Arms pulled back and eyes locked on targets, our classmates form a horizontal line. They remind me of warriors getting ready for battle, as they face black, blue, and red rimmed circles placed several yards away. Even the most fidgety kids stand still to concentrate before letting their arrows fly.

"Booyah!" Toby pumps his fist as his arrow hits the yellow center. "That's a bullseye! And ten points!"

Nathan and Carlos high five him.

"Beginner's luck." Chloe waves her hand as we pass. "I'll bet we can do better."

We take our place near a clear section of grass at the field's edge.

"Welcome to archery!" Jaimie walks over. "Let's get you set up with training. We only have three bows right now, so we'll take turns until I run to the main cabin for extras."

"How you doing, Trina?" He turns to her and smiles. "Have fun on this morning's hike? I found a wildflower patch I want to show you later."

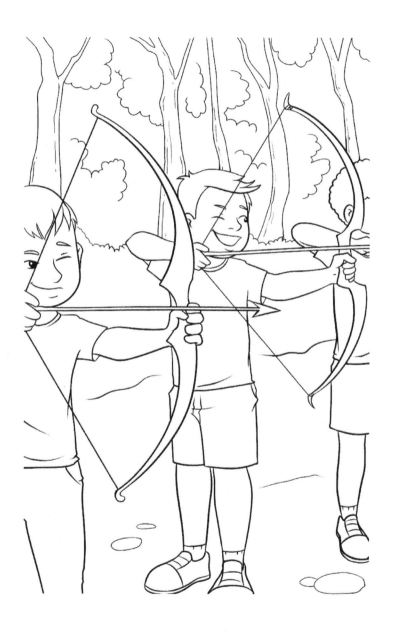

"I love wildflowers!" Chloe walks between them, fluttering her fake eyelashes. "Can I come too?"

"Uh, we'd need to check with your teacher," says Jaimie, looking flustered. "Okay, girls, let me demonstrate how to shoot a bow and arrow. We'll take turns until I get more bows."

"Let's see…how can we make this random?" He taps his chin with his finger.

"I know! Line up by hair length," says Trina. "I'll get the extra bows in the meantime. Be back in a sec."

"Yay! I'm first." Valentina walks to the front.

"I'm next," Carly swings her ponytail.

"And I'm third," says Christy.

My cheeks burn. I glance at Mariama, and she looks like a deer in headlights.

Trina's gone, and Chloe seems clueless. Should I say something?

Jaimie doesn't realize that Trina hurt our feelings by pointing out the differences in our hair. He gestures for us to imitate him, and we follow.

"There are five steps in archery. Number one: Line your body perpendicular to the target. Number two: Put your feet shoulder-width apart. Number three: Point your bow down and attach your arrow to the string. Number four: Point your bow toward your target. And number five: Aim and release."

"I did it!" Christy hits her arrow close to the bull's eye.

"Drat!" Valentina drops her arrow on step three and picks it up to try again.

Five minutes later, Trina comes back with extra bows and arrows for me, Mariama, and Chloe. I grasp mine like it's a piece of broccoli, and Mariama barely even looks at hers.

"Line your body up perpendicular? This is too much like math class," Chloe raises her hands helplessly. "Can you show me what to do again, Jaimie?"

Cupid has definitely struck its arrow in my best friend. She nearly faints as the counselor helps her hold her arms the right way.

"Is anything wrong, Sophie and Mariama?" asks Trina. "Why aren't you participating?"

"We don't feel like it," I answer. Mariama bites her bottom lip.

"Are you feeling well, Mariama?" Trina moves closer. "Hey, you're crying!"

She gestures for us to follow her to a side bench.

"What's up?" she asks gently. "Did anything happen in the cabin?"

I'm afraid to say anything, but when Mariama's face starts to crumble, I take a chance.

"Yesterday, some boys made fun of Mariama's hairstyle, and she felt bad. Then today, we were embarrassed when you made us line up by how long our hair is."

"Oh," Trina is quiet for a minute. "I'm so sorry to hear that I hurt your feelings. I had no clue this is an issue. Your hair is super cute, Mariama! Should I say something to the group?"

"I don't want to make a big deal about it with the other kids," Mariama shakes her head no.

"Okay, well please accept my apologies for this." Trina looks us both in the eye. "And let me know if any of the kids tease you again. I'm so sorry that I did something to make you feel bad, and I'll work hard not to make such a stupid mistake again. Both you girls are beautiful, and you have lovely hair."

"Thanks, Trina." I say. "I know you didn't mean anything."

"We probably need some diversity training here at Camp Glowing Spring," she says. "I'll suggest that at our next staff meeting. Are you all okay now? Would you like to try out archery?"

We nod and follow her back on the field with the others.

Chloe finished her one-on-one with Jaimie and is clowning around with Toby, Carlos, Nathan, and the other girls.

"Ready, aim, fire!" Toby makes the mistake of walking in front of Christy on the range, and she uses his backside as a target.

"No fair, I might get bruises." He rubs his rear and laughs.

"That's what you get for putting peanut butter in my shoe!" teases Chloe.

"Why would I do something that stupid?" says Toby. "I'm already on The Quacker's naughty list."

"Carlos has food allergies; there's no way we'd mess with peanut butter," Nathan adds. "It might send him to the hospital."

Valentina and Chloe look at each other in surprise. Could this be true?

"Hey, Chloe, something fuzzy's hanging off your eye." Toby gives her a closer look.

"Nothing's in my eye. What you talking about?" She turns her face to the side and rubs off the dangling false lashes. Mariama and I giggle.

I'm so focused on my friends that I almost miss a group of boys heading our way. Arnold and Brandon, from the cafeteria, are in the pack.

"Times up, losers! It's our turn." They boldly step to my friends.

"Who you calling a loser?" Toby slides forward.

Checking out his height and size, Brandon backtracks.

"No offense, Bro. It's just that it's our time to do archery."

"Says who?" Toby cocks his head to the side.

"Says the camp leaders." Arnold pokes out his chest.

The other boys beside him huddle in, ready for a fight.

I look around for the counselors. Jaimie and Trina are a few feet away laughing and shooting bow and arrows. Coach Quackenbush and Mr. Bartee are helping kids on the other end of the field.

"Leave us alone, you bully!" Mariama points her finger in Arnold's face.

"Not Puff Head again!" He curls his lips.

"What did you call her?" Toby leans over and balls up his fist.

"Leave it, Toby." Chloe puts her hand on his shoulders. "That jerk's not worth it."

"Yeah, he's one of the boys we told you about from lunch yesterday," says Christy.

"Do you kids need any help?" Trina and Jaimie interrupt the argument.

"These guys just ordered us to move." Nathan pulls his glasses off and puts them back on.

"It's our turn to do archery," Arnold repeats.

"Oops! He's right." Trina looks at her watch. "It's almost 1200. We should be heading over for lunch."

More kids from St. Regis crowd the grass, and Coach Quackenbush picks up his megaphone.

"Archery is officially over for Xavier. Line up to go to the cafeteria."

"You guys shouldn't be running around on your own," Jaimie turns to Arnold, Brandon, and their friends. "Didn't I see you out by the cabins earlier? Next time, wait for your assigned counselors to get you started on your activities."

"Yes, sir," Arnold answers.

When Jaimie turns his back, he and Brandon smirk and sarcastically wave goodbye to us.

"We should have told Jaimie and Trina that those guys called us names," huffs Christy, as we make our way off the field.

"If those fools mess with you all, again, just let me know," says Toby. "We have to stick together."

"Thanks, Toby. Save us a seat at lunch!" Chloe calls after him when Jaimie waves the boys into another line.

"That sure was nice of them to stick up for us out there," says Valentina.

"I thought you were mad at Toby for putting peanut butter in your shoe." Carly turns to Chloe.

"I don't think it's them anymore." She shakes her head. "Carlos has allergies."

"Well, if the boys didn't do it, then who did?" asks Christy.

CHAPTER EIGHTEEN

Operation Shaving Cream

"I bet those creeps from St. Regis put that peanut butter in our shoes!" Mariama says between a bite of her burger.

"Right...did you hear Jaimie say they were running around the camp earlier?" Carly points her finger in the air.

Lunchtime is nearly over, and we're still talking about our run-in with the St. Regis boys. My cabin mates and I gather around a rectangular table with Toby, Nathan, and Carlos.

Though we've only been here a day I'm already at home in Camp Glowing Spring's cafeteria. The juicy, grilled burgers are delicious. Nothing close to the hard, mystery meat they serve at Xavier. And we have a full hour to eat here, unlike the quick thirty minutes they give us at school.

"It's a good thing Jaimie and you guys' counselor came over," says Toby. "I was about to knock that big guy out."

"I'm glad you didn't do that because you would have just gotten into trouble," says Chloe. "And then we wouldn't be able to get them back like they deserve."

"Get them back?" I say. "What do you mean? We leave tomorrow, so hopefully, we won't see those boys again."

"I mean, that we're going to hit them with 'Operation Shaving Cream' today," Chloe says with a smile, and I inwardly groan.

"That's a great idea!" Valentina gives her a fist bump. "How do we do it?"

"What's 'Operation Shaving Cream'?" asks Nathan.

"A plan we had to prank you guys," Chloe says. "By giving you shaving cream mustaches and putting it in your beds."

"That's hilarious!" Toby slaps his knee. "We ought to put toilet paper around their cabin too."

"Or what about leaving some syrup?" suggests Valentina. "Then they'll get ants! Let's totally booby trap their room."

"Yeah, we'll show them!" says Christy.

"How will we find them?" I ask.

"That's easy," says Carlos. "Their cabin is just across the way from ours."

"I don't think this is such a good idea." I tap a French fry on my plate.

"Me either," says Mariama.

"What if somebody gets hurt?" Carly adds.

"How would we get hurt?" asks Chloe. "Don't be such babies, guys. This is going to be fun."

"Yeah, and they deserve it." Christy hits her hand on the table. "Look how they treated us."

I understand how she feels, and I kind of want to get back at them myself for almost making Mariama cry. But the retreat is nearly over, and I figure we should stay away from troublemakers. We don't know for sure if they pranked us, and if we're caught getting payback, Coach Quackenbush won't accept that as an excuse. I don't want to chance getting punished.

I'm also worried about running into that weird looking man I saw near the restroom and at the campfire. What if he's still on the loose?

It's like we're choosing sides in a battle as Christy slides to the other end of the table away from me, Mariama, and Carly. Nathan looks like he's not sure what to do.

The tension eases for a second when Trina rings a giant cowbell.

"Lunch is over in fifteen minutes, guys. Finish up and clear your tables so we can be out before the St. Regis group comes in."

"This is the perfect time to prank them." Toby slaps his palm on the table. "We have some free time before our next activity, and they'll be in here eating."

"Don't be such a worrywart, Sophie." Chloe puts her hands on my arm. "Come on. This'll be great."

"Count me out." I shake my head. "I'll see you guys when you get back to the cabin."

I stand up with my tray, and Mariama and Carly get up with me.

"I think I'll stay back in the room," says Nathan. "I've got some studying to catch up on."

"You're going to punk out too?" Toby purses his lips.

"Okay, suit yourselves." Chloe holds up her hands. "Come on, Valentina, let's hurry up so we can get the shaving cream. Meet you by the pine tree in ten minutes, Toby."

Our group goes back to the cabin together, and none of us says much. I feel bad that we are at odds with Chloe and the other girls, but I'm glad I'm following my heart. The camp housekeepers have left our cleaned shoes inside the doorway, and we put them on as soon as we get in.

"No hard feelings, bestie," says Chloe. "See you at 1345 hours!"

"That's 1:45 regular time," Mariama translates.

"Hasta la vista!" Valentina stands by the door and waves.

"Okay, be careful, guys." I gather them in a group hug.

"You act like we're going off to war or something," Christy giggles. "We're just pulling a prank."

I get a sinking feeling as they scamper down the path to meet Toby and Carlos. The other girls and I walk outside the cabin to hang out for a while.

"Thanks for staying with me guys." I turn to Mariama and Carly.

"No problem." Mariama shrugs her shoulders. "I'm not happy about what those bullies did either, but I figure we should just stay away from them."

"That's cool how Chloe didn't get mad about you not going," says Carly. "You guys are good friends. I thought there'd be a big blow out when you stood up like that."

"Hey, look over there, guys!" She stops talking and points at the pines. "There's a deer in the woods.

Awesome sauce! I wish we'd seen it when we were doing the scavenger hunt!"

I squint to see what she is talking about and notice something big shuffling through the trees on the same path our friends took. It's not a deer; it's the man who looks like Big Foot!

CHAPTER NINETEEN

The Prank

"OMG, it's Big Foot!" I cry. "He's going after Chloe, Valentina, and Christy in the woods!"

"But Big Foot is fake," Mariama shakes her head. "That thing we saw at the campfire last night was a counselor playing a joke."

"Does that look fake to you?" I point as the tall, wild-haired man takes a bite of something and throws it over his shoulder towards us. It thunks at our feet, and we shuffle backwards.

"Ewww! An apple core!" Carly steps away from the browning fruit.

"Big Foot loves apples!" I remember Cole's note. I wish I could see if his eyes are green like Cole mentioned on the list.

"Should we go for help?" whispers Carly.

"That might be too late." I gesture as the man disappears into the woods. "We've got to warn the other kids ourselves."

"This way!" Mariama points to a different path. "Remember that shortcut Trina showed us when we got here? If we go in this direction, we can get to the St. Regis cabin before he does."

"Come on, guys, let's go!" I run full speed ahead through the woods. I feel like a superhero as I rush to save my friends.

"Isn't Big Foot nocturnal?" Mariama huffs beside me down the winding path.

"That's what the show I watched said," I answer. "But he must come out in the daytime too."

"Watch out!" Carly waves at a hanging branch, and I duck.

"Be careful, so we don't get hurt," warns Mariama.

Five more minutes and we reach the St. Regis cabin.

"Awesome-sauce! It looks like it's snowing!" Carly exclaims.

Toby, Carlos, and Christy string toilet paper from trees like tinsel. Thin white paper hangs from most of the low tree branches and carpets the grass. I'm impressed at how much they have gotten done in such a short time.

"We have to get out of here, guys! Big Foot is coming!!" I yell. "Where's Chloe and Valentina?"

"Big Foot? What are you talking about?" Toby looks at me like I've lost my mind.

"Where are the other girls!?" Mariama shrieks.

"Inside the cabin spraying shaving cream," Christy walks over with an almost empty roll of toilet paper in her hand. "The cabin was locked, so they climbed in through the window."

"That man's coming!" Carly points to the clearing, where the trees are now rustling.

"Who's that?" asks Carlos. My stomach cramps.

"Take them back to their cabin, guys!" I wave to Mariama and Carly. "I've got to get Chloe and Valentina out of there!"

Realizing that someone is moving our way, Christy, Toby, and Carlos follow Mariama and Carly down the path we came from. I climb the step ladder up to the window and peek my head in. "Chloe! Valentina! Someone's coming! We've gotta go."

Chloe rushes to the windowsill with shaving cream smeared on her cheek. "Are you sure? We're almost finished."

"Yes, I'm sure! Come on!" My heart beats in my chest like a drum.

Chloe squirts foam under the covers of one of the bottom bunks, and Valentina throws the shaving cream can in the trash. "Operation Shaving Cream" is a success.

My two friends skid toward the window, and I suck in air. "Go out the door! I'll meet you there."

"Ahhhhh!" The kids outside scream. There's a clatter, and my feet swing underneath me, as the step stool falls.

"Chloe! Valentina! Help!" I scream. "I can't get down."

"Here you go!" There's a scraping on the ground, and Chloe adjusts the stool. I hop my foot on the step and thud to the ground.

"Are the other kids gone? Where is that man?" I look around wildly and rub my ankle.

"Dunno," answers Valentina. "I didn't see anything."

"No one was here when we came out," says Chloe. "The boys and Christy are gone."

There's no sign of our other friends or Big Foot. Toilet paper rolls lay on the ground.

"Are you sure someone was coming here?" Chloe crosses her arms.

"Yes! That tall, hairy man from the campfire followed you. We rushed over to warn everybody, and he showed up while you two were inside the cabin. I told Mariama and the other kids to go back to their rooms. I hope he didn't catch up with them."

"Well, come on then, let's find out." Chloe waves us over to the path, and we start running.

If Big Foot doesn't get us, I'll sleep like a rock again tonight. We've gotten plenty of exercise on this retreat. Sweat drips in my eyes, and gnats smack my skin as we jog along the dirt trail.

"I wish I could see the look on those St. Regis boys' faces when they get in bed," says Valentina with a laugh.

"That will be hilarious," snickers Chloe. "There's a full can of shaving cream in their sleeping bags. I'm glad we paid them back."

They aren't concerned about what Big Foot could be doing to our other friends. I don't know if what we saw is man or monster, but I do know that he spells trouble.

"Whoa!" I trip on a gnarled root on the ground and hold onto a nearby tree branch to keep from tipping over.

"Watch out, chica!" Valentina steadies me, and we slide the rest of the way through the gravel to the end of the trail.

Once we make it to the clearing, we're speechless. The other girls from our cabin stand with Trina and Jaimie. Scowling next to them is a barefoot man with a beard and straggly long hair who's at least seven feet tall.

CHAPTER TWENTY

Tug-of-War

"You need to do a better job of controlling these kids!" The giant growls to Trina and Jaimie. "They were near my cabin, and anything could have happened."

Up close, he looks more like a retired professional basketball player than Big Foot. He's taller than any person I've ever seen in person, with bright, green eyes, a beard, and sandy brown hair that reaches his shoulders. And the baggy, uniform he wears has a Camp Glowing Springs logo on the front pocket and is made of dark brown canvas like we saw hanging from branches on our hike.

"You're right, Darryl, and we're so sorry." Trina turns to us with a questioning look. "Why were you girls in the woods?"

"Um...we were exploring the trail." Chloe shifts her weight from side to side.

"Then we ran into your friend," I point to Darryl. "And we got scared that he was the ghost we saw at the campfire."

"Going out in the woods by yourselves is dangerous," says Jaimie. "I warned you about that when you came to camp. You could have been injured or hurt by some of the wildlife."

"We should have told you the whole story about Darryl after the campfire." Trina wrings her hands. "He's a ranger here in the park. His showing up during the ghost story was purely an accident. Darryl was in the woods restocking the firewood pile while we made s'mores."

"The special effects were so awesome when he came up on us in the dark that we didn't explain it," says Jaimie. "I should have realized you kids would try to figure it out. I'd better head back to the boys' cabin to make sure they're where they're supposed to be, Trina. See you at the mud pit in about an hour."

Trina turns to Darryl and gives a quick smile. "Thanks for your help, and sorry again for worrying you."

"No problem, just doing my job," he answers. "The kids from this retreat have been running wild. I caught a couple of boys from that other school spreading peanut butter on cabin doorknobs earlier."

"I knew it!" exclaims Chloe. "Those St. Regis kids are who messed up our shoes."

"Well, they're clean, now," says Trina. "So everything's fine."

"Alright, looks like you've got everything under control here." Darryl salutes Trina. "I'll see you later."

"See you, Darryl." Trina waves. "Thanks again."

He turns and marches back into the woods, leaving a trail of extra-large footprints behind him.

"Guess you were right, Sophie." Chloe turns to me. "There *was* a Big Foot."

"Why don't you girls change into some old clothes and rest a bit before it's time for tug-of-war," says Trina. "I'll be right out here, so don't get any ideas about going A.W.O.L."

"Whew! That was a close one," Valentina flops on her bunk after we walk into the cabin.

"Yeah. I almost peed my pants waiting for you guys to get here," says Christy.

"What happened on your way back to the cabin?" I ask.

"That weird guy, Darryl, yelled and chased us down the trail," says Mariama. "He didn't see the boys in front of us; they took another short-cut to their cabin. I can't believe we got away with this!"

"Well, it's not over until we're on the bus to go home," I answer.

"You got to admit that whole thing was exciting," says Christy. "I felt like I was a character in a movie."

"To you, the world is a movie," Carly says with a laugh.

We play a hand of Uno, and then Trina comes in to get us. "Tug-of-war starts at 1500 hours. Don't wear anything you aren't afraid to get covered with mud."

"I thought this was optional," Chloe whispers. "Now they're acting like we don't have a choice."

"We better make sure we don't lose, so we aren't pulled into the mud." Carly puts on a baseball cap.

"I wish I brought something to put over my head too," says Mariama. "I won't be able to fix it if it gets dirty.

"No worries," says Trina. "If you get muddy, you can hop in the pool to rinse off before your shower."

My stomach flutters like it's full of butterflies when we get to the tug-of-war field. There's a rectangular pit in the center filled with mud that's about the size of two bathtubs. A long, thick rope rests beside it. I hope we don't get a mud bath today.

Trina joins Jaimie and Darryl on the outer edge to get the best view of the action. Kids from our school and St. Regis scatter like ants to form teams.

"There's Arnold and those other meanies," Mariama elbows me in my side.

They gather on the St. Regis half of the mud pool. Arnold wraps a red bandanna around his forehead, and Brandon smears black football grease under his eyes. Some of the girls in their group stretch their arms.

"They aren't playing," I say.

"I wonder if those St. Regis boys have checked under their bed covers yet?" giggles Valentina.

"Hopefully they won't notice their surprise until nighttime," Chloe responds.

"Let's do this!" Toby, Nathan, Carlos, and their other roommates, Jason, Finn, and Aidan, run over to get us.

"You sure we can take them?" Carly asks.

"Definitely!" Toby makes a muscle.

"We need you girls to get in front of the line," says Nathan.

"Now, wait a minute, now!" Chloe holds up her palms.

"You're always saying 'ladies first,' aren't you?" says Carlos. "The biggest people stay in the back, and that's me and Toby."

"We need a team from Xavier to line up, please!" Coach Quackenbush booms from his bull horn.

"Let's do this!" Christy and Carly run behind the boys.

"Dominate, Cabin 3!" Trina's voice sounds through the crowd.

Mariama looks at me, and we hurry to catch up with our friends.

I'm so hyped up I feel like I've run five laps around the school track. My spot on the line is nearest the mud pit, and Mariama is after me. Across the pit, Arnold glares and raises his fist.

"We're gonna put you in the pig pen where you belong!" he shouts.

"Who does he think he's calling a pig?!" Chloe rolls her neck.

"Don't listen to that fool," calls Toby. "Just pull!"

I wipe my sweaty hands on the front of my jeans a final time before grasping the rope to begin.

"Ready, set, go!" Coach Quackenbush screams through the bullhorn, and the tug-of-war is on.

"Go, Xavier!"

"Yay, St. Regis!" Screams from fans for both schools roar like a wind tunnel.

"Aaargh!" Arnold puts all his weight into heaving the rope. My feet slide forward as if a rug has been pulled out from under me.

"Pull, pull, pull!" Mariama shrieks in my ear when I start moving in a reverse moon walk.

"I'm trying." I grit my teeth, but keep sliding forward like I'm a metal file and the pit's a magnet.

Eileen braces herself on the other side, and I get a sinking feeling. In just a few seconds we'll be covered in mud.

CHAPTER TWENTY-ONE

Last Night

"Squat down low!" yells Nathan. "It gives us a center of gravity."

I poke my behind out like I'm sliding into an arm chair. The rough rope scrapes against my palms. I bet I'll get plenty of blisters.

"Arrrggggh!!"

Mariama digs her feet into the ground and growls like a mama bear protecting its cub. Her fight gives me a second wind. I feel no pain as I yank the rope with all my might. Leaning back as far as we can go, our team moves together like links on a chain. On the other side of the pit, the front of Eileen's sneaker dips in the mud.

"We got this!" screams Toby. "Pull!"

I feel like I've just awakened from a nap and eaten a bag of candy as I drag the rope with my friends. One last yank, and it's over for St. Regis.

"Ahhhhh!"

Eileen face plants in the mud, and the rest of the St. Regis team drops behind her like dominoes. Half their team is covered in goo.

"Yeah!" Toby, Nathan, and Carlos bump each other in the chest.

"Awesome-sauce!" Carly high fives Christy. They're so excited they nearly stumble into the pit.

"They got a free spa treatment!" Chloe points as St. Regis kids wipe mud off their cheeks.

Arnold grabs onto Brandon to rise up from his knees, and they both plop down again.

"You guys are trash!" he yells at his teammates, scowling like an angry bulldog.

"Way to go, Cabin 3!" Trina runs over to congratulate us. "I'm proud of you guys."

"At first I was nervous about doing the tug-of-war," admits Chloe. "But it was fun."

"And you all were worried about us losing." Toby flexes his muscles. "There was no way that was happening with me and Carlos on the team."

"And what about me?" asks Nathan.

"I gotta admit, you pulled your weight, Bro." Toby slaps him in the back. Nathan smiles like he got picked first for a P.E. team.

"We never got to talk to you guys after the prank," I say. "How'd you find that short cut to your cabin?"

"Nathan figured it out doing his math homework," Toby says looking sheepish.

Confused, we all look his way.

"I practiced finding shortcuts in the trails to study for my math test," Nathan explains. "calculating the distance, rate and time it would take to get from our cabin to some of the camp trails I saw on the brochure."

"One of Nathan's shortcuts helped us fake out Big Foot," says Carlos.

"Fantastico!" Valentia pumps her arms in the air.

"Yeah! That's super cool," Chloe agrees.

"Have any of the counselors said anything about the prank?" asks Carly.

"Jaimie told us somebody TP'd St. Regis' cabin when he picked us up," says Toby. "But he didn't seem too upset."

"I wish I could be a fly on the wall when they go to bed tonight," Chloe says with a laugh.

We spend the rest of the afternoon swimming in the lake. I jump off the Blob three times and also go down the water slide. That night, after a dinner of yummy cheese pizza in the cafeteria, we have one last campfire.

"I'm going to ask my Mom to buy marshmallows and chocolate, so we can make these ourselves at home!" Christy rubs her tummy after finishing off two s'mores.

"Me too, they're sooo good!" says Valentina.

Sitting cross-legged around the flames' warm glow with my classmates, counselors and chaperones makes the forest feel much less scary than it did yesterday. I'm sad this is our last night at Camp Glowing Spring.

"This has been the best two days ever!" I say.

Suddenly, a shadow about three times as tall as I am pops up in front of me, and I almost jump out of my skin.

"It's Darryl!" exclaims Chloe from the other side of the fire.

The other sixth graders stare curiously at the huge, bearded visitor. Like earlier, he doesn't have shoes on. But he looks friendly this time, with a big grin on his face.

"Instead of having our usual ghost story, we invited Darryl, the park ranger, to tell you about some of the animals he's seen in his eight years at Camp Glowing Spring," says Jaimie.

"Being a park ranger is a dream job for me," Darryl begins. "I feel more at home out here in the forest than anywhere else. As you might have noticed, I'm a little different looking than other people." He stretches up to his full height, and the kids around me twitter. "But in the woods, I can relax and be myself."

Darryl describes how he tracks forest animals like deer, raccoons, and possum to study them and teaches at a nearby veterinary school.

"Awesome sauce!" says Carly.

"Mind if I take a photo?" Coach Quackenbush pulls out his cell phone after the park ranger finishes. "I'd like to keep this for the retreat scrap book."

"Come on Sophie! Let's get in there!" Chloe hops up. "We'll have a picture with a real, live Big Foot!"

Cole is never going to believe this!

I stand up to join her and smile.

About the Author

Tonya Duncan Ellis is author of the Sophie Washington book series which includes: *Queen of the Bee, The Snitch, Things You Didn't Know About Sophie, The Gamer, Hurricane, Mission: Costa Rica, Secret Santa, Code One, Mismatch, My BFF,* and *Class Retreat.* When she's not writing, she enjoys reading, swimming, biking and travel. Tonya lives in Houston, TX with her husband and three children. She does not believe in ghosts or Big Foot.

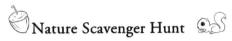 Nature Scavenger Hunt

Sophie and her friends have a fun nature scavenger hunt in the forest. Use this list to have your own nature scavenger hunt. Can you find all twenty?

1. Acorn

2. Animal Footprint

3. Bee

4. Berries

5. Bird

6. Butterfly

7. Cloud

8. Deer

9. Flower

10. Leaf

11. Lizard

12. Log

13. Moss

14. Mushroom

15. Pinecone

16. Rabbit

17. Rock

18. Spider Web

19. Squirrel

20. Tree Stump

Indoor S'Mores Recipe

S'Mores make a fun campfire or anytime treat. Try out these indoor kitchen s'mores recipes at home!

Ingredients

Chocolate
Graham Crackers
Marshmallows

Microwave Method

1. Place one graham cracker half on a paper towel. Top with a chocolate
bar half and marshmallow.
2. Microwave for about 10 seconds or until marshmallow gets puffy.
3. Top with other graham cracker half and press together.

Stove Method (Gas Stove)

1. Place one graham cracker half on a paper towel. Top with a chocolate bar half.
2. Using a long rod or metal skewer toast marshmallow over stove flame until lightly brown.
3. Place toasted marshmallow over the chocolate graham cracker half. Top with other graham cracker and press together.

Variations

1. Spread peanut butter on graham crackers before adding chocolate.
2. Add fruit (maraschino cherries, or banana or strawberry slices) on top of the chocolate.

FUN FACTS ABOUT BIG FOOT

Big Foot, a hairy, extremely tall, ape-like being who lives in the wilderness and leaves large footprints, has been a part of American and Canadian fork lore for years. Though considered a hoax, or joke, people continue to report seeing the mysterious creature. Check out these fun "facts" about Big Foot below:

- People report seeing Big Foot mostly in western Canada and the northwestern United States.

- Big Foot is described as weighing up to 500 pounds and being between six and nine feet tall.

- Big Foot gets its name from the enormous footprints it is said to leave, which are up to 24 inches long. That's more than twice the size of an average man's footprint!

- Another name for Big Foot is Sasquatch, which comes from a language spoken in British Columbia, Canada.

- Big Foot is said to be nocturnal, meaning it is most active at night. Big Foot's existence is still a debate because there is no physical evidence of the creature.

Books by Tonya Duncan Ellis

For information on all Tonya Duncan Ellis books about Sophie and her friends

Check out the following pages!

You'll find:

* Blurbs about the other exciting books in the Sophie Washington series

Sophie Washington
Queen of the Bee

Sign up for the spelling bee?
No way!

If there's one thing ten-year-old Texan Sophie Washington is good at, it's spelling. She's earned straight one-hundreds on all her spelling tests to prove it. Her parents want her to compete in the Xavier Academy spelling bee, but Sophie wishes they would buzz off.

Her life in the Houston suburbs is full of adventures, and she doesn't want to slow down the action. Where else can you chase wild hogs out of your yard, ride a bucking sheep or spy an eight-foot-long alligator during a bike ride through the neighborhood? Studying spelling words seems as fun as getting stung by a hornet, in comparison.

That's until her irritating classmate, Nathan Jones, challenges her. There's no way she can let Mr. Know-it-All win. Studying is hard when you have a pesky younger brother and a busy social calendar. Can Sophie ignore the distractions and become Queen of the Bee?

Sophie Washington
The Snitch

There's nothing worse than being a tattletale...

That's what ten-year-old Sophie Washington thinks until she runs into Lanie Mitchell, a new girl at school. Lanie pushes Sophie and her friends around at their lockers and even takes their lunch money.

If they tell, they are scared the other kids in their class will call them snitches and won't be their friends. And when you're in the fifth grade, nothing seems worse than that. Excitement at home keeps Sophie's mind off the trouble with Lanie.

She takes a fishing trip to the Gulf of Mexico with her parents and little brother, Cole, and discovers a mysterious creature in the attic above her room. For a while, Sophie is able to keep her parents from knowing what is going on at school. But Lanie's bullying goes too far, and a classmate gets seriously hurt. Sophie needs to make a decision. Should she stand up to the bully or become a snitch?

Sophie Washington Things You Didn't Know About Sophie

Oh, the tangled web we weave...

Sixth grader Sophie Washington thought she had life figured out when she was younger, but this school year everything changed. She feels like an outsider because she's the only one in her class without a cell phone, and her crush, new kid Toby Johnson, has been calling her best friend Chloe. To fit in, Sophie changes who she is. Her plan to become popular works for a while, and she and Toby start to become friends.

Between the boy drama, Sophie takes a whirlwind class field trip to Austin, Texas, where she visits the state museum, eats Tex-Mex food, and has a wild ride on a kayak. Back at home, Sophie fights off buzzards from her family's roof, dissects frogs in science class, and has fun at her little brother Cole's basketball tournament.

Things get more complicated when Sophie "borrows" a cell phone and gets caught. If her parents make her tell the truth what will her friends think? Turns out Toby has also been hiding something, and Sophie discovers the best way to make true friends is to be yourself.

Sophie Washington
The Gamer

40 Days Without Video Games? Oh No!

Sixth-grader Sophie Washington and her friends are back with an interesting book about having fun with video games while keeping balance. It's almost Easter, and Sophie and her family get ready to start fasts for Lent with their church, where they give up doing something for forty days that may not be good for them. Her parents urge Sophie to stop tattling so much and encourage her second-grade brother, Cole, to give up something he loves most—playing video games. The kids agree to the challenge but how long can they keep it up? Soon after Lent begins, Cole starts sneaking to play his video games. Things start to get out of control when he loses a school electronic tablet he checked out without his parents' permission and comes to his sister for help. Should Sophie break her promise and tattle on him?

Sophie Washington
Hurricane

#Sophie Strong

A hurricane's coming, and eleven-year-old Sophie Washington's typical middle school life in the Houston, Texas suburbs is about to make a major change. One day she's teasing her little brother, Cole, dodging classmate Nathan Jones' wayward science lab frog and complaining about "braggamuffin" cheerleader Valentina Martinez, and the next, she and her family are fleeing for their lives to avoid dangerous flood waters. Finding a place to stay isn't easy during the disaster, and the Washington's get some surprise visitors when they finally do locate shelter. To add to the trouble, three members of the Washington family go missing during the storm, and new friends lose their home. In the middle of it all, Sophie learns to be grateful for what she has and that she is stronger than she ever imagined.

Sophie Washington
Mission: Costa Rica

Welcome to the Jungle

Sixth grader Sophie Washington, her good friends, Chloe and Valentina, and her parents and brother, Cole, are in for a week of adventure when her father signs them up for a spring break mission trip to Costa Rica. Sophie has dreams of lazing on the beach under palm trees, but these are squashed quicker than an underfoot banana once they arrive in the rainforest and are put to work, hauling buckets of water, painting, and cooking. Near the hut they sleep in, the girls fight off wayward iguanas and howler monkeys, and nightly visits from a surprise "guest" make it hard for them to get much rest after their work is done.

A wrong turn in the jungle midway through the week makes Sophie wish she could leave South America and join another classmate who is doing a spring break vacation in Disney World.

Between the daily chores the family has fun times zip lining through the rainforest and taking an exciting river cruise in crocodile-filled waters. Sophie meets new friends during the mission week who show her a different side of life, and by the end of the trip she starts to see Costa Rica as a home away from home.

Sophie Washington
Secret Santa

Santa Claus is Coming to Town

Christmas is three weeks away and a mysterious "Santa" has been mailing presents to sixth grader Sophie Washington. There is no secret Santa gift exchange going on at her school, so she can't imagine who it could be. Sophie's best friends, Chloe, Valentina, and Mariama guess the gift giver is either Nathan Jones or Toby Johnson, two boys in Sophie's class who have liked her in the past, but she's not so sure. While trying to uncover the mystery, Sophie gets into the holiday spirit, making gingerbread houses with her family, helping to decorate her house, and having a hilarious ice skating party with her friends. Snow comes to Houston for the first time in eight years, and the city feels even more like a winter wonderland. Between the fun, Sophie uncovers clues to find her secret Santa and the final reveal is bigger than any package she's opened on Christmas morning. It's a holiday surprise she'll never forget!

Sophie Washington
Code One

Girl Power!

Xavier Academy is having a computer coding competition with a huge cash prize! Sixth grader Sophie Washington and her friend Chloe can't wait to enter with their other classmates, Nathan and Toby. The only problem is that the boys don't think the girls are smart enough for their team and have already asked two other kids to work with them. Determined to beat the boys, Sophie and Chloe join forces with classmates Mariama, Valentina, and "brainiac," Rani Patel, to form their own all-girl team called "Code One." Computer coding isn't easy, and the young ladies get more than they bargain for when hilarious mishaps stand in their way. It's girls versus boys in the computer coding competition as Sophie and her friends work day and night to prove that anything boys can do girls can do better!

Sophie Washington
Mismatch

Watch out Venus and Serena, Sophie Washington just joined the tennis team, and she's on her way to becoming queen of the court!

That is until her coach matches her with class oddball, Mackenzie Clark, and the drama really begins....Mackenzie refuses to talk to Sophie or learn the secret handshake she made up. Sophie just can't figure her out. Then Mackenzie starts skipping practice, and gets sick at school, and Sophie realizes that there's more to her doubles partner than meets the eye. Can Sophie make things right with Mackenzie before their first big game, or is their partnership a complete mismatch?

Sophie Washington
My BFF

You've Got A Friend In Me

Sophie and Chloe have been best friends since they met in kindergarten. They get along like chips and salsa and do everything together from playing tennis to cheering on the school cheer squad. Lately, Chloe's been leaving Sophie out, and she doesn't know why. Sophie does everything she can to make her best friend happy, but it's not working. Then Chloe asks Sophie to fib to a teacher to help her out and she learns the true meaning of friendship.